MY DAUGHTER'S HUSBAND

DANIEL HURST

www.danielhurstbooks.com

Download My Free Book

If you would like to receive a FREE copy of my psychological thriller 'Just One Second', then you can find the link to the book at my website *www.danielhurstbooks.com*

PROLOGUE

What is it about my daughter, Ellie? Why does she seem to be drawn to such dangerous men?

Or is it simply that they are drawn to her?

I put the first time down to bad luck. Daryl, my daughter's former boyfriend and the charming Californian, turned out to be deadly, but I stopped him just in time. After that, I figured there would be no more dramas in my daughter's love life, barring the usual things like her getting upset that somebody she likes hadn't texted her back or a new partner leaving the toilet seat up and annoying her with that simple domestic grievance.

Honestly, I was looking forward to things being far simpler going forward with my child's romances than they had been in the past.

Lightning couldn't strike twice, could it?

I assumed not, and when Ellie told me that she had met a new man, while I did feel a little anxiety, I told myself that this time would be different, which was why I made sure to welcome the handsome, charming male into my home. It's also why, after only six months of the pair dating, I gave my blessing for my daughter to get married to her new lover.

At the point of his proposal, it had been five years since Ellie had endured a torrid time at the hands of her dangerous American lover. She had matured, gaining experience in all walks of life, and that was why I felt confident that her getting married and settling down was not only the right thing for her but the best thing too.

A white wedding. A perfect honeymoon. The stability of a home together. And then, in time, a new addition to the family, a little boy or girl to brighten up my daughter's life and a little grandchild for me to love, someone who could keep me on my toes just as much as my own offspring had as I grew older.

At least that was the plan I made in my head. But things tend to be perfect there, don't they? We don't make imperfect plans in our dreams, we make ones where everything works out well in the end. Unfortunately, that is not real life, and dreams don't always become reality. What's more, as I have recently discovered, to my horror, *lightning can strike in the same place twice.*

My daughter's American boyfriend was a nightmare. But my daughter's English husband is no different. Two men, both liars and both secretly wanting to bring harm to my child.

Why must I always find out so late?

Maybe the first time, despite it all, I got lucky. I found out just in time and because of that, I was able to stop him before he hurt her. But what about this time?

I have a feeling I'm too late.

This is different. Last time, the dead body of my daughter's boyfriend meant things were over.

This time, the dead body of my daughter's husband means things are only just beginning.

How do I know that? It's because I currently have no idea where my daughter is. What I do know is that at the moment, as his body is being taken away, the police are looking at Ellie as a possible suspect in the death of her husband.

But they're also looking at me.

What is going on?

Where is my daughter?

Is she still alive?

And why, after her boyfriend, did her husband turn out to be just as dangerous?

BEFORE

1

DAWN

All anybody wants on their wedding day is a little bit of sunshine. I know my daughter is no different, and that is why she and her husband-to-be have opted to say their vows in a place that practically guarantees blue skies and warm temperatures.

Rather than take their chances with the unpredictable and often disappointing British weather, the soon-to-be-wedded couple asked all their guests to join them on a hot July day in sun-kissed Turkey, a place with a climate that makes a mockery of England's wet and windy summer months.

As I stand on this hotel balcony in Antalya, looking out over the calm, blue waters of the Mediterranean, I am struck by how different this is to my own wedding day many years ago. When I put on my white dress and walked down the aisle to marry the man of my dreams, it was a frosty winter's day in Suffolk, England, my home county and the place where I decided to get wed simply because it was the cheapest option. The concept of marrying abroad and asking family and friends to board a plane and fly overseas was not really around then, or at least not for people who had a whole lot of love but not a whole lot of money. While I would have liked nothing more than to have been married with the sun on my back and a view of the yachts bobbing around on the sea in front of me, the reality was that Sean and I just wanted to tie the knot in as simple and as cost-effective a way as possible. So that's what we did. We said our vows in the church where my parents said their vows years before me, and then we went to the function room at the local leisure centre where we all overindulged in cheap champagne and even cheaper canapes, and that was it. We didn't even have a honeymoon because Sean had to be back at work on a building site, and I had a shift of my own to get to, though that was fine by us because we knew what we were building towards.

We already had our own home, a modest, semi-detached property that was small but cosy.

What we wanted was a family to help fill it even more.

Rather than blow all our budget on our wedding day, we kept some cash in reserve for the baby we hoped to have.

Nine months after our wedding night, Ellie was born.

I'll never forget the sight of my daughter when a midwife handed her to me in that hospital room after a gruelling labour with Sean by my side. But I have a feeling that I'm not going to forget what she looks like when I see her in a moment either and that's because I'm eagerly anticipating getting to see her in her white dress.

I look back to the glass doors behind me, but Ellie has not emerged yet, which must mean she is still inside and allowing her make-up artist to put the finishing touches to her appearance. But that's okay because a quick check on the time tells me that we still have ten minutes until she is due to walk down the aisle.

Leaning over the balcony, I can see the terrace below, upon which the wedding will take place, and that's how I know that everybody else is already in position. I can see the top of all the guests' heads, the males in smart suits and the females in colourful dresses, and I bet many of them are glad this ceremony is taking place in the morning rather than later in the day when the sun will be higher and the mercury in the thermometer will be too. But by the time the temperatures could be getting uncomfortable here, they'll all have retired inside to the air-conditioned room where the food and drinks will be consumed, the speeches will be made and plenty of dancing will be done as the sun begins to set.

Looking down from the balcony at the gathered guests, I don't quite count everybody in attendance, though it wouldn't take me too long if I wished to do so. That's because this is quite a small ceremony, and the number of people here is a result of a few different things. Ellie and I are part of a small family, so we didn't have loads of cousins or aunts and uncles to invite, which would have boosted the numbers. Ellie also has quite a small friendship group - two best friends who are also preparing backstage in their matching bridesmaids outfits. My daughter is similar to me in that regard, preferring a smaller circle of friends over a larger network of various acquaintances, and as I look down, I see two of my friends in their seats. Ellie very kindly invited my mates, Maggie and Tanya, so that I would have some company during the day while she was busy with all her duties, and I'm glad the two women accepted the invites and flew out here for a bit of a holiday. But they're not simply here to make up the numbers because, as my oldest friends, they have known Ellie since she was born, and in a way, they are like aunties to my daughter, albeit not in the traditional bonded-by-blood sense.

While it's pleasant to have my two best friends here, there is one woman who could have been sitting in a seat beside them if only she had chosen to do things differently. That would be Kirsty, my third best friend, or at least she was until she decided that she would sell her story to the newspapers after the whole thing with Ellie's American boyfriend happened five years ago.

I'll never forget seeing the story on the front pages of the papers in which she divulged intimate details about Ellie and me, offering up personal facts that added colour to the story of how the pair of us could have easily died at the hands of Daryl, Ellie's dangerous partner from LA. She cashed in on her connection to us, putting finances before friendship, and I have not spoken to her since. That is why I can never forgive her for allowing it to happen, and that is why she is not here now, basking in the warm sunlight. She's back in the UK, and the last time I checked the weather app, it was raining there.

Ha.

Moving my gaze on from my two friends, I look over the rest of the guests, though there aren't many because, like his bride, the groom also has a small circle of loved ones. In fact, that is an understatement because he has even fewer people than Ellie. There's one elderly man in attendance, who is the father of the groom, and then there is a guy in his thirties who is the best man, and that's it.

The groom himself is standing where he should be, at the altar beside the registrar, and he looks dashing in his smart, black suit. He also looks a little nervous, but that is understandable. It's not every day that a person gets married, and I know he'll be anxious that things go smoothly. But I'm sure they will, just like I'm sure Ellie is marrying a good man here today.

As everyone continues to wait for my daughter to make an appearance, I think about how happy the man she is marrying today has made her in the short time they have known each other. It was only six months ago when Ellie told me that she had started dating somebody, and it's only been four months since I first met him. But like everybody who meets Kyle Beaumont, he made a big impression on me from minute one.

Tall, dark, devastatingly handsome but with the politeness and humour to offset his good look so that he could never be accused of veering towards arrogance, Kyle is a confident, successful but humble man. At thirty-two, he's three years older than Ellie, and the fact that my daughter is due to enter her thirties herself in the next twelve months is enough to make me feel very old.

Well, that and the fact that I'll be turning fifty in the next year as well.

Not letting age get in the way of a good time, I brush off thoughts of how quickly my life seems to be flying by and am just about to turn to look back at the double doors in the hope that Ellie might be ready when I hear a voice behind me.

'What do you think, Mum?'

The sound of Ellie suggests she is all set for her big moment, and when I turn around and see her, I get confirmation that is the case. That's because I see my baby girl looking radiant in a flowing, white dress, and the sight of her looking like a princess in one of the bedtime stories I used to read to her as a child is all it takes for tears to well up in my eyes.

'Oh my goodness, you look beautiful,' I cry as I approach the blushing bride, only the tears I'm trying to contain blurring the magnificent view of my gorgeous girl.

'Do you think so?' Ellie asks, clearly not quite as sure herself, but there is no need for her to doubt her appearance because she looks incredible, just as I knew she would.

'Honestly, you look amazing,' I say as I delicately wipe my eyes and pray that my mascara won't smudge, though I have opted for a water-resistant kind on account of how many tears I expect to shed during the course of today.

'Is everybody ready?' Ellie asks me then, but before I can answer, one of the staff members at this venue comes to tell us that everyone is in their seats and ready to go. I know I could tell Ellie to take a quick peek over this balcony, and she would see the guests for herself, but I don't because she would also see Kyle then, and I think it would be more magical if she first saw him as she was walking towards him down the aisle.

'Are you ready to get married?' I ask my daughter, tears once again disturbing my vision, and

Ellie looks nervous as she nods her head before we make our way inside and go downstairs to where the bridesmaids are waiting. The two glamorous friends wearing all pink are just as thrilled to see Ellie in her dress before we all take our positions for the ceremony to begin. That means all I have to do now is link arms with my daughter, and we are ready to go.

As my right arm interlinks with Ellie's left, I think about how I'd give anything for her father to be in my position now. Sean, my late husband, should be the one doing this because it's every dad's dream, but sadly, fate conspired against us all there. It's been nine years now since he succumbed to a tumour and was cruelly taken away from us both in the prime of his life, but as we have done every day since his passing, mother and daughter have been by each other's side and bravely facing whatever else life throws at us. The tragedy of losing her father when she was just twenty caused Ellie to distance herself from me, and our relationship was extremely strained for a while. But we were brought much closer together after what happened in America with her boyfriend and his father five years ago, and while it was a shame it took as much as me saving my daughter's life to re-establish our bond, it's now back to being unbreakable.

As the music begins to play and the bridesmaids walk ahead of us, Ellie and I step out into the sunlight and prepare to face our audience. Whilst doing that, I make sure to stay fully present in the moment and savour every second of this happy occasion, not just because it will go quickly but because there was a moment when I feared I would never get to experience it.

Daryl, Ellie's infamous American boyfriend, tried to kill my daughter and almost succeeded, before I killed him and saved her. He only got so close to doing so because his father, Harvey, covered up his son's previous crimes and, ultimately, went to prison for him.

He was a parent who would do anything for their child, and that's a tale as old as time.

But while Harvey lost his son and paid for his crimes, my child is still alive and deserves all the happiness that is coming her way.

As for Harvey, that handsome American man who welcomed me into his home in Los Angeles once, he has no one to blame for his current situation but himself.

As far as I know, he's still in a California prison serving out his sentence for perverting the course of justice.

Long may it stay that way.

2

HARVEY

'Prisoner 6723588-A, step forward, please.'

I recognise the combination of letters and numbers that make up my prisoner ID, so I follow the command and move one step forward to get closer to the warden standing in front of me. Once I am, another warden approaches me from behind, and as he gets to work on the handcuffs around my wrists, I know I am about to be relieved of them any moment now. After doing that, the two wardens march me along a corridor before I enter a room with a table, upon which is some kind of document and a plastic container that is full of things I recognise from my life before I became a resident here.

I see the clothes and shoes I was wearing when I was arrested, as well as my wallet, house keys and watch, along with a state lottery ticket I purchased from a convenience store just before my incarceration. I can't remember what numbers I chose, but it doesn't matter now because, after five years, I'll already be too late to claim any prize I might have won.

That would be just my luck to have won millions but have been too slow to get them. Then again, there are more important things in life than money. I'm wise enough to know that, as well as wise enough to realise that for today, luck is on my side, and I get confirmation of that when a man standing on the other side of the table from me tells me that all I have to do is sign the document beside my belongings and I will be free to go.

Not wishing to waste any more of my time, especially after having already lost so much of it, I say nothing as I pick up the pen and scribble my signature before turning to the items in the container. Picking up my wallet, I open it up and quickly thumb through it to re-familiarise myself with the items inside. I see my two credit cards, though both have expired now, as well as my driving licence and social security card. Other than that, there are just a couple of $20 notes, and that's it, though, thankfully, I have more money than that in my old bank account that I will soon be able to access after so long without withdrawing from it.

'You can take your belongings and get changed in there,' a warden tells me, so I pick up the container and enter a small room with a wooden bench fixed to one of the walls. It's there where I sit and get changed, gratefully peeling off the orange uniform that has been the only thing in my 'wardrobe' since I became an inmate here. I feel much more comfortable once I'm back in my shirt, jeans and white sneakers, and after fastening my watch around my wrist, all that is left for me to pick up is the lottery ticket.

I briefly glance at the numbers before stuffing it into my back pocket, and even though I know I might as well throw it away, I feel like keeping it, as if it is a memento of the free life I was living before everything changed and I ended up in handcuffs, spending my days surrounded by killers, rapists and thieves and wondering if I was even going to survive long enough to be a free man again. But I have survived my time in prison, and as I'm led towards a door that will take me back into the outside world, I briefly glance back over my shoulder for one last look at this place. The sight of the bars on the windows and the iron doors that would lead back to where all the crowded cells are is enough to make me never want to come back here again, and as the door ahead of me opens, I suck in the fresh air of the prison car park.

Being in Los Angeles, it wasn't too crazy of me to expect that I would be walking out to a beautiful, sunny day in Southern California. But that is not the case because the sky is heavy with dark clouds, and a little rain is falling onto the asphalt around me. However, the weather is not going to dampen my spirits, not now I am free, and as I walk towards the red car with the idling engine, I am pleased to see that my ride away from this place is waiting for me.

The driver of the vehicle is not a family member or friend because they all cut ties with me once I was convicted of my crime, and good riddance to them for all I care. No, the driver here for me today is the only person who actually stuck by me during my sentence, and they did that in the form of writing to me and visiting me throughout the five long years that I was locked up.

'Hello, Harvey. My, you look handsome today. It's nice to see you in your own clothes, though I must admit, I miss the uniform a little.'

I'm sitting in the passenger seat beside Clara, a woman who began writing to me not long after I was sentenced. The story of me and Daryl made huge headlines in America, but while most of the people who heard it condemned my actions, there were several people who saw things from my side and reached out to let me know it, calling me a good father and saying I was only doing what I could to protect my son. Most of them turned out to be slightly crazy, and I mostly felt amused at the desperate women, particularly the one in Seattle who proposed to me. But amongst all the nonsense, there was one letter that I enjoyed reading, and it was from Clara.

She wrote to me and expressed how she thought I was brave for doing what I did and that it showed what a good parent I had tried to be. That's what I believed too, which is why I wrote back to her, and the communication soon went beyond simple letter writing and reached the point where Clara was coming to see me every week during visiting hours. She professed her love for me one year into my sentence, and by then, I admitted to being fond of her too. She has stuck around ever since, keeping my spirits up during my prison experience until today, when I'm finally allowed to re-enter civilisation again.

'Thanks for collecting me,' I say, before glancing back at the prison walls. 'Let's get out of here.'

Clara is only too happy to hit the accelerator pedal, and as the prison shrinks in the rear-view mirror, she asks me where I want to go.

'My place or yours?' she enquires, and I get the sense that after so many years of simply expressing our mutual interest in conversation or handwriting, she would now like to express it in another way. I'm more than happy to do that; after all, it has been five long, lonely years with only other men for company, but there is something I'd like to do first.

'Take me to the cemetery,' I say, as I try not to feel a little overwhelmed by the sight of all the buildings, cars and pedestrians that make up this busy section of LA. 'I want to visit my son.'

Clara understands and navigates us to my preferred destination, keeping any disappointment she might have about us not yet being more intimate disguised and understanding that some things are more important than the two of us falling into bed.

Things like family.

As Clara tells me about how she has kindly delivered flowers to my son's graveside every week since we became close, I thank her, whilst also wishing that I could have been out here to do it myself. As it is, I have only been to my son's grave once, on the day he was buried, and even then I was wearing handcuffs and was flanked by several police officers.

As raindrops hit the windscreen and a storm closes in, making Los Angeles look less like a tourist destination and more like a place people would want to escape, I think about the chain of events that led to my situation now.

It all started when Daryl met his British girlfriend online. After he told me about the Englishwoman called Ellie, whom he had grown close to over the internet, he asked if she and her mother could come to visit us. Not wanting to stand in the way of my son's happiness, I said yes, and before I knew it, I was picking up Ellie and her mother, Dawn, from LAX. Things started off well between the four of us, and as our children grew closer, Dawn and I bonded over the fact that we were single parents, having both lost our partners over recent years. But then things took a turn when, after the English pair left my home abruptly and returned to England, an anonymous tip-off was made to the LAPD in which Daryl was highlighted as a possible suspect in the disappearance of Aubree Parker, a young American woman who had been missing for some time in Los Angeles. With the police at the door, my son panicked and confessed everything to me. He had killed Aubree, a girl he had gone to school with, before burying her at a private spot in the desert, the same spot where I proposed to his mother years earlier. In order to send the police to us, Daryl figured that Dawn had found the photo of him with Aubree that was taken at our house not long before she went missing and while no one before had known she was with us that day, they knew then.

After confessing that he had killed her, my son left me with two options.

I could hand him over to the police officers who were knocking on our front door.

Or I could be a real father and help him.

I chose the latter, mainly because I understood that my son got his violent tendencies towards women from me. Unbeknownst to him, or anybody else to this day, for that matter, I killed Jodie, my wife and Daryl's mother, poisoning her and getting away with it several years ago, so it was clear to me then that my son had inherited my violent tendencies towards women. The only problem was that he hadn't covered his tracks as well as I had, so in order to deflect attention away from him, I told the police that I was the one who had hurt Aubree and to prove it, I took them to her burial spot in the desert.

While I went to prison, it allowed Daryl to stay free, and I advised him that he had to be more careful in the future. He assured me he would, although he soon made a mockery of that because he travelled over to England to rejoin Ellie. Thinking that he was no longer a threat because I had pretended it was me who was the real danger to women, Dawn and Ellie welcomed my son into their home, only for Daryl to reveal his true character and try to kill Ellie in a park one night. Sadly for him and for me, Dawn was able to save her daughter at the last second and killed Daryl before he killed Ellie.

At that point, people were starting to question the honesty of my earlier confession, so I admitted the truth – that I had covered for my son in Aubree's case and wasn't really her killer after all. That admission was accepted, though I still wasn't able to walk free because I had to be re-sentenced - this time for perverting the course of justice and delaying the truth from reaching Aubree's family. But a five-year sentence was much more preferable to a lifetime one, and now it's over, I can start looking forward instead of back.

I'm a free man now, and the first thing I want to do is visit my son's grave.

The second thing I want to do is take revenge on the two women who helped put him in there.

Dawn and Ellie might think that after five years, what happened in the past is over.

But they're wrong.

It's not over, not by a long shot.

It's only just starting.

3

DAWN

I've never felt particularly self-conscious before but that has quickly changed now that everybody on this terrace is looking in my direction. However, even though it feels like all eyes are on me, in reality, they are on the woman walking beside me.

Glancing to my right, I see Ellie looking resplendent in her dress as we make our way along the aisle. But she is also looking a little nervous too. That's why I whisper to her, reminding her how beautiful she looks, and her smile grows a little bigger as she approaches the man she is about to marry. As for that man, his smile couldn't be any wider than it is right now, and as we reach Kyle at the altar, he has the look of a guy who can't believe his luck. But if he was in any doubt as to his privileged position, I whisper something to him as well, before leaving the happy couple.

'Take good care of her,' I say, partly as a way to tease him as if I'm the scary mother-in-law who will be watching his every move. But I'm not that, so it's just a bit of fun. But the other part of me that wanted to say it is keen to express the symbolic nature of what I have just done.

I've essentially given my daughter away to him. No longer am I the most important person in the world to my child. That is now him, and while I can't say my parenting duties are officially over, because they never will be completely, this is another big step towards Ellie needing me less in her life as she begins to build a family of her own. That realisation, combined with the fact that her dad is not here to see how gorgeous our daughter is looking, is why my tears quickly return, and this time, there is no stemming the flow.

Fortunately, Maggie and Tanya, my two dependable friends, are quickly on hand with the tissues, and I take them before dabbing at my eyes and then finding my seat. As the few gathered guests sympathise with my teary display, the registrar begins proceedings and as he does, this setting couldn't be more perfect.

The view that Ellie and Kyle have as they exchange their vows is astonishing - the sea stretching out endlessly before them, just as endlessly as the love they share for one another. The crazy thing is that this wedding didn't even cost as much as it would have done if it had taken place in England. Wedding fees back home are astronomical, and what do those who are paying get for it? They certainly don't get a view like this, that's for sure, nor are they likely to get this calming sea breeze in their faces. I can now see why Ellie was so keen to have her wedding here. It was actually Kyle who suggested Turkey, and at first, I had a few reservations, even though I knew I wouldn't get the final say if it came down to it. But I did remind my daughter that it was stressful enough to organise a wedding locally, never mind one hundreds of miles away. But Ellie quickly warmed to the idea of having the ceremony somewhere sunny, and once that was decided on, all they had to do was pick a date.

It might have felt like a bit of a hassle having to board a plane and fly for four hours to get here, my wedding attire in tow, and all while trying to keep a nervous bride-to-be calm, but now we're here, I can see that it is worth it. And besides, a four-hour flight is much shorter than the eleven-hour flight I took to Los Angeles the last time Ellie let her heart venture out beyond the English border.

Back when she was dating Daryl, and before it turned out that he was a psychopath, I was convinced that Ellie was going to end up moving to America and I'd only ever get to see her once or twice per year at best. Of course, in hindsight, I'd have accepted that fate much more than the one that actually transpired. But with that in the past and Ellie having met her new man, I can't say it's not brilliant that they both plan to stay in England and even better that they'll be living within driving distance of me.

Kyle already has his own place, a sizeable house in the nice part of our hometown, and Ellie is currently living there with him. I think their plan is to stay there, and that plan is fine by me because it's only a fifteen-minute drive from my house and is not far from the supermarket where I work, meaning I can call around for a cup of tea with my daughter whenever I can. It'll also help to be close when I'm asked to perform babysitting duties at some point in the future, but one thing at a time.

As the vows continue, I hear both Ellie and Kyle clearly and confidently confirm to their guests that they will support and cherish each other forever and be there for one another, no matter what lies in store for them and their marriage in the future. Then, once all the formalities are out of the way, the registrar very loudly and proudly has a declaration to make.

'Congratulations. I now pronounce you husband and wife!'

Those words are sealed with a kiss between the happy couple and met with rapturous applause from everybody around them, and after witnessing my daughter tie the knot, I couldn't be any happier. I also feel like I need a drink because it's already been an emotional day, and it's not even noon yet, which is why it is a relief to see somebody making their way around with a tray of full champagne glasses.

'To Ellie,' Maggie says after we have all taken a glass, and we clink our drinks together before taking a cool, refreshing sip from the fizzy bubbles.

'Gorgeous ceremony,' Tanya adds. 'Just wonderful. You must be so proud.'

'I am,' I confirm as I watch a photographer leading the happy couple to the edge of the terrace, where they will have their photo taken with the breathtaking backdrop behind them. I'm sure I'll get called over soon to have some photos with the bride and groom, which I can't wait for, but for now, I'm happy to sip champagne with my best friends.

'Kirsty really missed out here,' Maggie says. 'I bet she regrets selling her story now. Yeah, she got some money and built an extension on her home for doing it, but so what? True friendship is priceless, and she doesn't have that anymore.'

I smile at Maggie, and it goes without saying that I am grateful to both her and Tanya for choosing my side over Kirsty's after she spoke to those journalists and made a tough time even tougher in the aftermath of what Daryl did.

'I'm so happy for Ellie,' Tanya adds. 'After what she's been through, she deserves all the joy in the world.'

'She sure does,' I say, and before I know it, my champagne glass is empty, and I'm already looking for another one. But before I can find it, Tanya has something else to say.

'You know who else deserves to be happy? You do,' she says to me, and Maggie agrees enthusiastically. 'Which reminds me, any progress on the dating front yet?'

Oh no. Here we go again.

I should have known it wouldn't take long for my friends to bring up the subject of my love life. That's because it has been one of the main topics of conversation for a while, although, to be fair, it has been a while since I lost my husband, and many people would have already moved on by now. Nine years and counting, and I still haven't been on so much as a single date in all that time. But Maggie and Tanya are determined to change that.

'You're still so young,' Maggie has told me on several occasions, and while I always reply by reminding them that my next big birthday is my fiftieth, Tanya always tries to tell me that "fifty is the new forty," whatever that's supposed to mean.

'Maybe you could meet somebody here,' Maggie muses as she looks around. 'A nice Turkish waiter, perhaps. Some toyboy you could bring back to England. That would be fun.'

She winks at me, and I'm not sure if she thinks it would be fun for me or fun for her and whatever fantasies she likes to entertain whenever she's bored of her husband.

'No, forget about Turkish toyboys,' Tanya chips in. 'What you need is a good old-fashioned English gentleman who has a bit of money and can pay to treat you well, just like Ellie has got for herself. I think that when you get home, you should try and find one. I know you've always resisted dating sites, and I accept that many of them are just full of pervy men who only want one thing. But there are some good ones out there. A woman in my spin class met a very dashing man in his fifties who treats her like a queen, always taking her away for long weekends in the countryside. He even bought her a new car.'

I roll my eyes as my two friends excitedly discuss what kind of guy I might end up with, be it a young man who can go for hours in the bedroom or an older guy who has the bank balance to give me a life of luxury. But whatever they are thinking about, the fact is that none of it can happen unless I make the decision to give dating a try.

Do I even want to?

The answer to that question has always been no, but being here and being reminded of what it is like to be in the presence of love, I can't help but think I perhaps should have another go at romance. I'm not saying I want to get married again, but with potentially another thirty or forty years ahead of me, it seems like a long time to not even see who might be out there as a future companion. Even more so now that Ellie is going to need me less. I'm going to need to find something to fill my spare time with when I'm not working, and while running errands for my daughter and dealing with whatever dramas have been consuming her life have taken up a lot of my days since she was born, I have a feeling Kyle is going to handle all those things now, leaving me sitting around at home and wishing I had a strong male figure of my own to lean on.

Maybe it's the champagne going to my head, or maybe it's the heat because it is getting hot out here on this terrace, but whatever it is, I decide to tell Maggie and Tanya that I will start dating when I get back home. Unsurprisingly, both women are delighted at that news, though I temper their enthusiasm by emphasising how it will only be when I am home so they don't start running around Turkish hotels looking for somebody to pair me up with.

Fortunately, I'm pulled away from my friends when Ellie calls me over to have a few photos taken with her and Kyle, so I rush over to join my daughter and her smiling groom, and the three of us pose for several pictures with the sea glistening over our shoulders.

This day is going as well as I hoped it would, and nothing can spoil it, not even a little rain, though that is unlikely here.

I feel sorry for anyone who is under an umbrella and a dark sky today.

They have no idea what they are missing.

4

HARVEY

The rain is pitter-pattering against the top of the umbrella I'm holding as I make my way towards the gravestone that sits amongst hundreds of others in this sprawling cemetery in North LA. Clara is beside me, and I'm grateful to her for bringing an umbrella so that we wouldn't get wet as we go to pay our respects at my son's resting place. But the closer I get to his headstone, the darker my mood becomes, and I'm at the point where the energy in my body is feeling as black and heavy as the storm clouds that are currently sitting above the City of Angels.

'Hello, son,' I say as I reach Daryl's grave and stare at the lettering inscribed onto the headstone. They are letters that I had commissioned, instructing the person who made this headstone on what to write so that the deceased currently lying in a box beneath it would be remembered how I wanted him to be remembered.

A loving son with a good sense of humour and a fierce determination to get what he wanted.

That's the Daryl I knew.

I don't care what anybody else thinks of him because nobody knew him better than me.

Certainly not the journalists who have written so many articles about him and especially not all the members of the general public who have formed an opinion about him and decided that he was simply evil. I get why they think that, though. As far as they are concerned, he killed Aubree Parker and tried to kill again when he attacked Ellie in England, so it does seem like he had a bad side. I'll admit that he had his issues but a killer is not all he was, and I want to make sure that is made clear, which is why this headstone tries to do that. Unfortunately, sometimes a member of the public sees it fit to try and vandalise this grave, spraying graffiti and destroying any flowers that get left here. Clara has told me about it, and while she has always made an effort to clear it up, it keeps happening.

Screw them vandals. They think they can destroy the memory of my boy, but they are wrong.

They're also wrong if they think that Daryl's story is over yet.

I'm going to see to it that it's not.

'The Aggies won yesterday,' Clara says to the grave, referring to my son's high school football team in Texas, one he was proud to support during his time at university there. '20-17. It was a really good game. You would have enjoyed it.'

I appreciate Clara saying something like that because she is right; Daryl would have enjoyed it if he had been alive to watch it, and there is no doubt in my mind that he should have been. He should have been around for a long time yet, another fifty or sixty years at least, so there would have been a lot of football games to watch and enjoy. I'm also aware that he should have been the one visiting my grave, not the other way around, because that's the natural cycle of life.

The parents go first, the kids last.

But not in this case.

Dawn saw to that.

'Could I have a private minute alone with him?' I ask Clara. 'You can have the umbrella.'

I offer it to her because it seems unfair of me to make her go and stand in the rain without it, but she declines, pointing out a large tree at the edge of the cemetery and telling me she'll seek shelter under there until I'm ready. Then she gives me a kiss on the cheek before jogging away to escape the bad weather, leaving me alone, huddled under the umbrella and standing over my son's final resting place. Now we are alone, I can speak openly to my boy.

'I'm not going to let them get away with what they did to you,' I say to Daryl, praying there is some way he can hear me in the afterlife. 'I have a plan, and while I'm not exactly sure it is going to work, I promise you that I will do everything in my power to try.'

The rain gets louder on my umbrella, but I don't allow it to deter me from saying what I came here to say, and I keep talking as if my son is standing right in front of me and I am looking into his face.

'I'm going to go to the UK, and I'm going to visit Dawn and Ellie,' I say, free to express my criminal plan with Daryl because he can't report me to the police. 'I'm going to go as soon as I can because every second they are alive is an insult to me and your memory.'

My head is filled with visions of Dawn and Ellie laughing and smiling and living a good life in England, and they are visions that have haunted me throughout my time in prison. The thought of them enjoying each other's company - that special parent-child bond that I have lost - makes me furious, and I can't wait to bring it to a stop. Of course, while I have been incarcerated, I have no idea what that pair have been doing with their lives, but I assume they are thriving, whatever they are up to, and thinking they are only fuels my need for revenge even further, which can't be a bad thing.

'Unfortunately, now that I have a criminal record, I can't simply just catch a flight to the UK,' I go on, spelling things out for my son as if he really is a part of my revenge plot and not just worm food below this wet soil. 'Anyone who spends over twelve months in prison can't just fly in and walk through passport control over there in England. So, to avoid the risk of being sent back to America without getting to do what I need to do, I'm going to take a detour.'

The thought of the long journey that stretches ahead of me is a slightly overwhelming one, but I have no other choice. It's either go or stay here and let Dawn and Ellie get away with things, and if I did that, how could I ever come back to this grave and tell my son that I had tried my best for him?

'I'm going to have to fly to a European country first - one that has lesser laws about allowing convicted criminals through their borders. The Netherlands might be my best bet,' I say. 'I can fly there with my criminal record, and once there, it's not too far from England then. Of course, there's just the small matter of getting across the sea into England, but I'll figure something out.'

While I'm still not exactly sure how I will do it when I get there, I am aware of people being smuggled into the UK every day by various modes of transport, so I will have options. Whether or not any of them will work is another matter, but as always, I will try.

'But this means that while I might be able to get there, I'm not sure how easy it will be for me to get back,' I add as the rain only intensifies. 'This may end up being a one-way mission and if so, I won't be able to come and visit you again.'

I look up at Clara standing underneath the large branches of the tree several yards away and see that she is staying mostly dry over there. I also know that she is totally oblivious to the plan I have just voiced, and I intend to keep it that way. I don't need her knowing that I will shortly board a flight to Europe because I doubt that she'll be happy about the fact that she has supported me throughout my sentence, only to see me leave her not long after getting out of prison. I have no idea how she might react to that, and if she's angry, she may decide to go to the police and if she did, they could tell Dawn and Ellie that I am coming for them. It's best to keep Clara in the dark about my intentions, which is why, as far as she knows, we'll be starting a life together very soon here in LA.

But Daryl knows what I am really going to be doing.

'I will try my best to make this right,' I say to him in closing. 'I promise you that.'

Then I kneel beside the grave and reach out to place a hand on the cold, wet headstone.

'I love you, son,' I say, meaning it deeply.

Then I stand up and walk away, not looking back because I'm telling myself this won't be the last time I will be here. I'll succeed in my plot and make it back to LA. I won't die in England like Daryl did. His body had to be repatriated, but not mine. I'm going to be coming home and when I do, I will be back here to tell my son all about how well things went. I'll be able to describe in graphic detail how I ended the lives of Dawn and Ellie. I'll be able to recite the horrified expressions on their faces when they see that I have come back for them. And best of all, I will be able to tell Daryl how much they begged for mercy just before I silenced them forever, making sure that they knew that, ultimately, it was my family who had got the better of them and not the other way around.

'Are you okay?' Clara asks me when she sees me approaching the tree, and I nod my head before welcoming her back under the sanctuary of the umbrella.

'I'm fine,' I reply as we walk towards the gates that lead to the car park. 'Let's get out of this rain.'

Clara agrees with me there, and after she suggests we go back to her place, adding a cheeky wink to really let me know what she has in mind when we get there, I agree with her that it sounds like a good idea. But really, there are only two places I am interested in going next.

Very shortly, I will need to go home, returning to my house that has stood empty for the past five years, and when I get there, I will pack my clothes and pick up my passport before walking out the front door. Then I will go to the airport and buy a ticket that will allow me to fly out of the country and, in the process, significantly close the gap between me and the mother and daughter who I despise so much.

Dawn and Ellie have no idea that I am coming for them.

But the clock is ticking now.

Best of all, only I know it.

5

ELLIE

It's my wedding day, and so far, so good.

I have already walked down the aisle and while that was nerve-wracking, it was mostly just a blur of smiling faces, so I didn't have too long to stay anxious about that. I have also said my vows, not tripping over any of the words and making it through that part of the day without a hiccup. Since then, I have smiled for lots of photos, eaten a lovely meal and drank one or maybe two more glasses of champagne than I perhaps should have. But all that is okay. What is making me nervous now is the fact that the speeches are due to begin any minute and when they do, that will be the one part of this event that I don't have full control over.

While I'm not making a speech myself, my new husband is, and I'm trying to tell myself that he won't say anything embarrassing about me. Kyle doesn't look nervous at all about the fact that he will be standing up shortly and talking to our guests, so I suppose that's a good thing, but what is he going to say? I'm not the first bride who has worried that her groom will overshare details of his relationship, and the last thing I want is anything too awkward to be said by him about me, especially when my mum is in attendance. So that means no sex stories. No bathroom habits. Nothing that can make me cringe or blush or cover my face in shame. Those are the rules, and I have told Kyle that, but will he stick to them as he promised, or will he be like all those grooms I have seen making speeches in videos online? He knows the ones - the kind who think they are stand-up comedians and share what they believe to be hilarious anecdotes, only to end up embarrassing their bride and half the people in the room at the same time.

As I see somebody approaching our table with a microphone, I guess I'll find out soon.

But before he can get his chance to speak, there is somebody else who will be making a speech before him, and as I watch them receive the microphone and get up from their seat, I am also wondering what they are going to say.

It's time for Mum's speech.

As the room falls silent, I think about how it should have been my father, Sean, who was preparing to address the room now. Tradition states that the father of the bride makes a speech on his daughter's wedding day, although in my case, that is not possible. But just because I've lost him before his time, it doesn't mean he hasn't been present in my thoughts all day, and I know he's been very present in Mum's too. I'm sure I'll get even more evidence of that when she starts speaking, so in preparation, I reach for the packet of tissues that I strategically placed on this table in the expectation that I would be shedding plenty of tears during this part of the day.

'Thank you all for coming here today, and thank you to all the wonderful staff at this lovely venue who have been looking after us during this wonderful wedding,' Mum begins, politely addressing both our guests and our hosts in one smooth sentence. Then she turns to me and my new husband and beams at us.

'What a beautiful couple. Let's toast to Ellie and Kyle,' she says, raising her champagne glass, and everyone follows suit.

Okay, so this is going better than expected. No embarrassing stories about me as a baby yet.

'When Ellie was a little girl, she used to have a favourite teddy bear,' Mum says next, and I immediately cringe.

Oh no, here we go.

'The bear was called Pink Pink,' Mum says, and everyone in the room laughs and finds it cute, while I just hide my head in my hands. 'And Pink Pink was Ellie's best friend when she was little.'

Did you really need to bring this up, Mum?

'Ellie would take her everywhere with her, and she would sleep with her too. She also used to tell her all her secrets and worries, but what Ellie didn't know was that Pink Pink would then report back to me if there was anything I needed to know.'

A few people laugh while I just wince because I have no idea where this story is going, but it surely only ends in embarrassment.

'Of course, teddy bears can't actually speak, so Pink Pink didn't really tell me what Ellie was saying to her. I had to find that out by secretly standing on the other side of her bedroom door and listening in when Ellie didn't know I was there.'

I shoot Mum a look because I had no idea that she had done such a thing, but Mum just smiles back at me.

'As any parent knows, kids won't tell us everything, so we sometimes have to resort to sneaky tactics to find out what is on their mind,' Mum goes on. 'Anyway, while I was listening in one night, I overheard Ellie telling Pink Pink about some of her hopes and dreams.'

Oh no, what embarrassing thing is Mum about to recite now? I dread to think, but a five-year-old's hopes and dreams can't be anything but embarrassing, right?

'And do you know what I heard?' Mum asks her captive audience. 'I heard my daughter telling her favourite teddy bear that one day when she was all grown up, she was going to get married to a handsome prince and have a fairytale wedding. Well, here we are. I guess that dream came true.'

Everybody in the room loves the story, and I have to admit it is pretty sweet, so I smile at Mum whilst hoping she will move on to another topic now. But she's not quite finished yet.

'Do you know what else I heard?' she asks everyone. 'I heard Ellie tell Pink Pink that when she got married, she wanted her favourite teddy bear with her on her big day.'

Oh no.

'So guess what?' Mum cries. 'Here she is!'

With that, Mum reaches under the table and then produces Pink Pink herself, my little pink teddy bear that

I haven't seen for many years and who I had no idea Mum had kept all this time.

As everyone in the room claps their hands and laughs, I feel my face getting hot and wonder if I'm turning as pink as my beloved teddy bear herself.

Mum is smiling at me and clearly thinks she is both hilarious and cute, and I can't help but admit that it has been funny, but I am also relieved when I see her put Pink Pink down, and Mum moves on to something else. However, the next subject is almost as uncomfortable for me, though in a very different way.

'Of course, there is somebody who should have been here today who couldn't be, and that is Ellie's father, Sean,' Mum says, and I note the crack in her voice as she speaks and wonder if she is going to cry like I already am. 'Sadly, Sean passed away when Ellie was twenty but before he did, he gave me something.'

Mum takes out another surprise then, and this time it is a letter. Then she begins reading it and as she does, it's impossible for me to stop the tears flowing down my cheeks.

'My dear Ellie. If you are listening to this, congratulations, you found somebody to marry you. Good luck to whoever that poor guy is.'

I didn't know it was possible to cry and laugh at the same time but everyone, including me, manages it.

'I'm so sorry that I'm not with you to share in your special day. I would have loved nothing more than to have walked you down the aisle and given you away to the groom, if only because giving you away would mean you were now his problem and not mine.'

More laughter.

'But seriously, Ellie, I really wish I could be there today to see you start this next exciting chapter of your life. I'm sure you look beautiful, and if I know one thing, it's that the man sitting by your side is now the luckiest guy in the world.'

Kyle takes my hand and gives it a squeeze while Mum wipes away a few tears from her eyes before continuing to read.

'I'll wrap things up now because nobody likes a wedding speech that goes on for too long, especially when the person who has written it is a dead guy,' Mum says, before shaking her head at her late husband's dark humour. *'I just wanted to say, dear Ellie, that I love you and wish you many happy years of marriage, just like I had with your mother.'*

Mum is really crying now and struggling to finish, so I stand up and put an arm around her for support, giving her the strength to compose herself and go on.

'Just remember two things for a happy marriage. If the husband thinks he is right, then he is wrong, and if the wife thinks she is right, then she is.'

More laughter, and with that, Dad's pre-written speech is over, leaving me and Mum to hug tightly while everybody stands and applauds the touching moment.

After such an emotional thing, it takes me a minute to compose myself and remember that the speeches aren't over yet, and now my husband has the microphone in his hand and is ready to go.

Trusting that Kyle's speech will be a warm and light-hearted one that draws admiring smiles from its audience rather than a debauched, X-rated one that draws gasps of shock, I brace myself for what he has to say. He starts by referring to Sean, and that is very kind of him, before moving on to me and, more specifically, how we met.

'It began like any good story in that it was a dark and stormy night,' Kyle says, drawing a laugh from the room, in particular from Mum's friends, Maggie and Tanya, who seem enamoured by my new husband, as many women seem to be because he is drop-dead gorgeous.

'I was avoiding the rain outside by sitting in a pub and having a drink when I saw the most beautiful woman walk in,' Kyle goes on. 'Anyway, she quickly left again before Ellie entered.'

I roll my eyes at the lame joke as Kyle chuckles to himself.

'I could tell that you had just come inside to get out of the rain as well because you were soaking wet, and I felt a little sorry for you as you went to the bar and ordered a drink,' Kyle says. 'When I saw you go and sit down by yourself at a table, I really wanted to go and talk to you, but I didn't have the courage, even after a second beer. But when I saw you finish your drink and get ready to leave the pub, I knew it was now or never. So I went for it.'

I smile as I think back to the night when we first met, and while it was true that the weather was awful and I only went into that pub that night to avoid the rain, it ended up being the best thing that ever happened to me.

'Knowing that you didn't have an umbrella but seeing that it was still raining outside, I quickly grabbed mine and followed you out of the pub,' Kyle recites. 'Then I offered the umbrella to you so that you would stay dry. Do you remember that?'

'Of course,' I whisper to Kyle as I smile at him standing beside me.

'You didn't want to take my umbrella, so I suggested we walk under it together, which we did, and ten minutes later, after I'd walked you to the bus stop, you had given me your phone number, and despite the weather, I was feeling like the happiest guy in the world.'

'It pays to be a gentleman,' I say, and everyone laughs.

'It sure does. But what I didn't tell you was that the umbrella I used that night was not mine. I actually borrowed it from another guy in the pub, and once I'd left you, I ran back to the pub to give it back to its owner. Then I went home and was absolutely soaked by the time I got there. But it was worth it for your phone number.'

I had absolutely no idea that was the case and can't believe Kyle was using somebody else's umbrella that night. But now that I do know, it just makes it seem even more romantic because he was obviously eager to try and talk to me and because he did, we are here now.

'I love you, Ellie, and want to thank you for making me the happiest guy alive,' Kyle says, raising his champagne glass. 'I also want to promise you, Dawn, that I will treat your daughter as she deserves to be treated.'

Mum really appreciates that sentiment, as do I, because Kyle knows all about my torrid history with Daryl, so he knows how important it is that I don't have any more dramas in my love life going forward.

'Now, let's finish our meals, drink some more champagne and dance the night away!' Kyle cries, and everybody agrees with that, clapping their hands as Kyle retakes his seat beside me and gives me a kiss.

Those speeches were perfect, just like the rest of the day has been. What's even better is that Mum seems to be having a great time as well. Her tears have dried after her emotional reading of dad's letter, and a big smile is back on her face, and why wouldn't it be? I imagine a child's wedding day is one of the best days of a parent's life, and it's great to see Mum looking so happy after all she has been through.

She went through hell with Dad and his illness, and she went through hell when I inadvertently invited an American killer into our home, but now she can relax and enjoy her life again.

One thing I have realised is that when I'm happy, she is happy, which only tells me how much she loves me, and what's best is that I can't think of anything that could spoil my happiness now.

Nothing at all.

It really feels like as far as my life is concerned, the best is yet to come.

And it is, right?

6

HARVEY

The rain is still falling in Los Angeles, and I can see precipitation on the window from where I'm currently lying in bed. But my view of the outside world is temporarily blocked when the woman I am lying with raises her head and repeats her question, clearly because I wasn't listening properly the first time she asked it.

'Harvey? What do you think of my idea?'

'Your idea,' I say, confused because my mind is a million miles away from this bedroom in Clara's house, the place we came to after leaving the cemetery earlier.

'Yeah. About the two of us living together. I know you've only just got out of prison, and I don't want to rush things if you need more time, but it would be nice if we could wake up next to each other every day, wouldn't it?'

For a woman who has spent the best part of five years either writing to me, reading my responses and visiting me, not to mention most of today with me in person, Clara seems to have absolutely no idea that the last thing in the world that I want to do is settle down with her in either her house or mine. It's not that she isn't pleasant company, and waking up next to her every day would be quite nice, particularly if we end up doing a lot more of what we have just done when we got into bed for the first time. But sadly, I'm going to need a lot more than just companionship to make me happy these days.

The quiet, settled-down life is not for me.

The only thing I want is cold, cruel revenge.

Nothing more and certainly nothing less.

'Erm, yeah, it's a good idea. I'd love to live with you,' I say, almost speaking on autopilot because even as I answer, I'm thinking about Dawn and Ellie rather than the naked woman with her arms intertwined with mine.

'Great!' Clara cries before putting her head back down on her pillow and allowing me to see the rain-soaked window again. Perhaps it's the unseasonable weather in LA that is making me feel so low today, or maybe it's because I know that every second I spend here with Clara is a second I am wasting getting on with what I really want to be doing.

'So what are you thinking? Do you want to live here, or do you want to go back to your place? I'm happy with either. I don't care as long as we are together,' Clara goes on, but I cut her short there before I carry on committing to things that I have no intention of seeing through.

'I'm sorry. I'm really tired. It's been a long day. Hell, it's been a long five years. Can we talk about this tomorrow?'

'Oh, yes, of course, I'm sorry,' Clara says, genuinely apologetic as she gives me a kiss and then begins stroking my hair as if to try and relax me further. But that won't cut it.

'I need to go home, just for a short while to get some things and check on the place,' I say. 'If you don't mind, I'd like to go alone. Just because I think it's going to be a lot to deal with being back there without Daryl, and I need a little private time. Do you understand?'

'Of course I do. Take as much time as you need,' Clara tells me. 'I'll be right here waiting for you to get back.'

I thank Clara for her understanding before getting out of bed and quickly getting dressed. It takes me longer than I'd like it to for me to locate all my clothes, mainly because Clara threw them all over the place when she was hurriedly removing them earlier.

Five years felt like a long time for me to be without the company of a lover, but as Clara proved, it was the same for her.

'I'll see you tomorrow,' I say once I'm finally dressed, and Clara tells me that she can't wait, which is nice of her, although I refuse to allow myself to feel too guilty about the fact that this is most likely going to be the last time she will ever see me. That's because once I walk out of her front door, my revenge mission will begin in earnest, and there is simply no place for her in what happens next.

This next chapter of my life is going to be unpredictable and messy.

There's also a chance it could be my last.

After declining Clara's offer to drive me home by saying I need some fresh air and a bit of exercise so I'd prefer to walk, I leave her place and make my way along the rain-soaked streets that lead me back to a main road. Once there, I hail a taxi and give the female driver my destination before settling into the back seat and double-checking in my wallet that I have enough money for my fare. I don't know exactly how much the cost of taking a taxi has gone up since I've been off the streets, but I can see the meter as we drive on and figure I've got enough on me to cover this.

As I stare out of the window and see numerous palm trees swaying in the breeze with swirling clouds above them, I am hoping this bad weather won't be affecting flights out of LAX. The last thing I need is to be delayed any further, and I'm hopeful that by this time tomorrow, I'll be in Europe after spending most of the night in a plane cabin at 38,000ft. But that remains to be seen because I won't know how quickly I can get there until I get to the airport. For now, I just need to get home, get packed and then get going again.

'I'm sorry. You might get this a lot, but I feel like I recognise you from somewhere,' my driver suddenly says, her eyes on me in the rear-view mirror. 'Are you an actor?'

I'm aware that I am an actor of sorts, though I doubt it's in the way the driver is thinking of me as. But rather than have her realise that she recognises me because my image was on all the TV news channels in this city when my son and I were making headlines for all the wrong reasons five years ago, I do a bit more of the kind of acting that LA, and Hollywood in particular, is known for.

'Yeah, I'm an actor,' I lie, with a shrug.

'What might I have seen you in?' comes the next question.

'I've done a few commercials, nothing major.'

'That's cool! I'm trying to get into acting myself.'

I can't say that's a shock because knowing what this city is like, it seems that half the people here are working actors and the other half are wannabe actors, and as my taxi driver asks me for any tips on how to break into the industry, I offer her a few lazy platitudes like 'just keep trying' and 'never give up' before I'm relieved to see my house come into view.

As the driver thanks me for the acting tips I gave her, as well as for the cash I hand over for my fare, I exit her vehicle, slightly amused that she really has no idea who she has been driving around today. She probably thinks I've been in toothpaste or dog food commercials, but better that than having her know who I really am and what I've done.

As she drives away, her head no doubt filled with starry dreams about making it big in Tinseltown, I look at the home I haven't seen inside for so long. It's not exactly good to be back, not when I'll be walking in alone. Nor will I ever hear the sound of my son's voice filling the rooms inside again as he asks me to watch a football game with him. But at least I still have a place to call my own, and as I approach the front door, I'm grateful that I'd already completed my mortgage on this house before my sentence, meaning there was no chance the bank could have foreclosed on me for late payments while I was in prison.

Turning the key in the lock, the door is a little stiff when it opens, but that is to be expected because these hinges haven't been used in a long time. The mail that has been pushed through my letterbox hasn't been collected in a long time either, and I stare down at the pile of envelopes by my feet and wonder how many of these letters are legitimate things I need to read and how many of them are notes from people who hate me and my son and have decided to write to me telling me what a horrible person I am. But I'd rather they write angry letters than smash my windows or graffiti the exterior walls of the house, which is what I was told was happening during the early days of my sentencing. I was able to have it arranged so that any damage was repaired, and the trouble seemed to die down in the end, but I am betting some of these envelopes contain messages from people who want to tell me what a horrible person I am for trying to cover up my son's crimes in the past.

Whatever. I bet many of them would do the same if their child broke the law and they had a straight choice between helping them or confining them to a prison cell for the rest of their lives.

Opting not to go through all the mail yet, I leave it by the door and walk around the rest of my home, checking on all the rooms to make sure everything is as it should be. There's plenty of dust but other than that, everything looks the same. It's like stepping into a time capsule and seeing my life as it was five years ago before it all went wrong.

Before Dawn and Ellie came here and messed everything up for us.

Opening the sliding doors that lead onto my patio, I step into my back garden and look at my swimming pool. The water inside is green with algae, a consequence of it not being treated for so long, but as I stare at the pool, all I can see is the memory of Ellie swimming in there with my son back when they were dating. Then I look at the table and chairs to my left and recall me sitting there sharing drinks with Dawn as the pair of us watched our children playing in the pool and remarked on young love and how wonderful a thing it could be. I liked Dawn back then; she had a humility about her that told me she was an honest person. I trusted her, and I guess she trusted me too because we had some nice conversations, or at least she did until she decided that she and Ellie had to leave and return to England, and I have not seen either of them again, at least not in person anyway.

But as I go back inside and head upstairs to my bedroom, I am intent on seeing them soon, and after finding my passport in my safe, where it was left years earlier, I shove it into my jeans pocket before pulling out a rucksack from under the bed and then tossing on a few essential items that I'll need during my travels. As always, it doesn't take me long to pack for a trip, and once I'm done, I carry my case downstairs and place it by the front door, not far from all the letters that I'm most likely never going to get to read now. That's because as I take one more look around my house, I expect this will be the last time that I'm ever here. Then I pick up my case and walk out of the door.

Next stop the airport.

I'm most likely on a suicide mission here, but that's fine by me.

Last time, Dawn and Ellie came to me.

This time, I'm going to them.

7

DAWN

While the travel time from Turkey back to England has not been enough to give me jetlag, I am still exhausted as I go about my daily routine now that my daughter's wedding is over, and I have been home for twenty-four hours.

In that time, I've done all the usual things a person does after getting back from their travels. I've unpacked my suitcase and washed all my dirty clothes, as well as completed any errands that need doing around the house, like sorting through the mail, doing some tidying up and buying groceries to replenish the empty fridge. That latter job required me to make a trip to the supermarket, which is not something I always relish, considering I work in that same supermarket, meaning a trip like that just feels like more work to me, even if I'm not wearing a uniform when I go shopping. But at least I get a staff discount on any items I purchase there, and the trip also gave me the opportunity to see a few of my colleagues, all of whom were eager to know how Ellie's overseas wedding went.

It was hard to keep the big smile off my face as I excitedly told them all about how well everything had gone and how beautiful my daughter had looked on her big day. It might have even seemed like I was exaggerating at one point with how enthused I was about the proceedings, but the truth is that everything went absolutely perfectly, and it was everything I could have hoped for to see Ellie made so happy. I made sure to show them a few photos on my phone to prove that I wasn't exaggerating at all, and they all confirmed that it looked incredible. But like all good things in life, it had to end at some point, and with the wedding over, I am very much back to reality as I move around my home, tidying up, getting ready for my return to work tomorrow and most of all, cursing the bad weather outside because it means I can't put my washing out to make it dry quicker.

That sunny day in Turkey, when I walked Ellie down the aisle, seems a long time ago now, but at least my daughter hasn't had to come back to reality just yet. She is still in that hot country with her new husband, and while I am due to pick them up from the airport when they get back soon, at least they have been able to extend their happiness for a little while longer.

It's tradition for a couple to have their honeymoon just after their wedding, but Ellie and Kyle haven't quite followed that trend, although it's mainly because of work commitments rather than a desire to be different. Kyle runs his own business, and despite trying, he was simply unable to take too much time away from work, meaning a full-length honeymoon was not possible so soon after their big day. But he has assured Ellie that they will do something in the near future, and a trip to the Maldives has been mooted, so I'm sure my daughter can exercise a little patience when there is such a tantalising trip on the horizon for them soon. However, while Kyle was eager to return to England after the wedding so he could get back to work, Ellie, quite rightly, in my opinion, said they should have at least a couple of days to themselves before returning to normality, where it would be just the two of them enjoying each other's company abroad. Kyle eventually conceded, and that is why the pair are still soaking up the sun in Turkey, lounging by a pool and sipping strong drinks instead of being back here looking out at this rain.

I know that they are by a pool with a drink in their hand because Ellie has been sending me lots of photos, but I'm not envious of her and the fun she is having while I'm here trying to get my washing dry. That's because, as any mother knows, I am happy if my child is happy, and I can certainly see that is the case where Ellie is concerned.

Entering the kitchen and checking on the latest load of clothes that are currently going through a spin cycle in my washing machine, I pass the fridge but briefly pause when a photo catches my eye, stuck to the fridge door beneath a Mickey Mouse magnet. It's the one of me, Sean and Ellie at Disneyland, taken years before my husband got sick and Ellie was robbed of her doting dad.

As always when I see the photo, I pause and reflect on a happier time, as well as think about what might have been, because there is no doubt my life would have been very different if Sean was still here to share it with me. Instead of being in this house alone, he would be around here somewhere too, possibly in the living room watching sport on the TV, or maybe he would be being a little more useful than that and helping me with all this washing.

Yeah, right - I know there would be more chance that he'd have his feet up with a beer than be fiddling around with the washing machine.

But I don't care because I'd give anything just to have him here still. I'd also give anything to have been able to add a new photo to the front of this fridge, one in which Sean and I were standing proudly beside our daughter in her wedding dress because that would have been an incredible image to add to our family archives. As it is, the photo of Ellie in her dress only has me in it, not Sean, though I will still add it to this fridge once I've gotten around to printing it off and putting it up here.

Suddenly feeling a little too melancholy to be doing housework, I take a seat at my kitchen table and pick up my mobile phone. I've spent most of the time using it to look at the photos I took in Turkey ever since I got home, but now I'm using it for something else.

I'm using it to do the thing I promised my friends I would do.

I'm downloading a dating app.

However, I'm not going to say that listening to my friends talk to me about the virtues of re-entering the dating pool is the thing that has persuaded me to do this. I'm my own woman and can make my own decisions, which is why I am doing this, not because anybody thinks I should do, but because I want to. Deep down, I know it is time for me to move on from Sean rather than allow the rest of my life to be lived reminiscing over a past that can never return. I don't have to put any pressure on myself and say that I'm looking for a new husband or anything like that, and if I'm honest, the thought of walking down an aisle again in a white dress of my own fills me with dread because it just seems like far too much work at my age, having already done it once before.

No, if I do this, I am doing it simply because it would be nice to have somebody to share things with, somebody who isn't Ellie or my best friends or my colleagues at the supermarket. I'm missing a male presence in my life, a strong but warm and gentle man, somebody who can make me laugh, challenge me in conversation, hold me when I need it and lift me up when I am going for something. A partner to go for dinner with, catch a movie together, go on holiday and sip drinks by a pool with.

Will I ever be able to truly fall in love again like I did with Sean in my youth? I'm not sure about that, but I probably owe it to myself to try, and I don't think doing so will in any way taint the memory of my late husband or make it seem like I am disrespecting the impact he has left on my life. He'll always be my Sean, but he's not here anymore, and unless I do something about it, I'll die alone in this house, and when Ellie talks about me at my funeral, there won't be anybody there to stand up and describe what I was like as a partner.

Unless I find somebody on this dating app.

I've never been particularly technological, which is why it takes me several minutes of playing around with the app until I feel like I have some semblance of an understanding of it. Having pushed multiple buttons and entered in several personal details like my name, age, location and dating preferences, I appear to have finished completing my profile. Oh no, wait, one more thing to do. I have to add a photo of myself so that any potential suitors can clearly see who it is they are interacting with.

The thought of having to find an image that I feel best represents me and my ageing appearance is a daunting one, so I spend an awfully long time trawling through the photos on my phone to see if I can find something that might be in some way appealing to a member of the opposite sex. It's tempting to use an image that was captured several years ago when I was looking a little more youthful than I appear now, but that wouldn't be very honest of me, and it would only lead to disappointment on the part of any of the dates who turn up to meet me if they were expecting somebody who looked ten years younger. Then again, how many of the men who make themselves available for selection on this app are misrepresenting their appearance? I bet there are a few, and I wouldn't be surprised if I was to go on a date with a man who has a full head of hair in his profile picture only to discover that he's totally bald in person. But so what? I'm not superficial, and I would never disregard somebody purely on the basis of looks.

Hair, no hair, fat or thin, tall or short - I'm looking for a loving and loyal companion, not a model.

I only hope the people looking at my profile can say the same, or they'll be very disappointed.

Finally settling on a photo of me that was taken a few months ago when I went for lunch with Ellie, I upload it and am pleased with how it looks. In the image, I am smiling and appear youthful but not so youthful as to be deceptive, and with that, my profile is complete.

In terms of my preferences, I have made my selections and have indicated that I am looking for a man between the ages of 45 and 55 who has shared interests in things like watching films, going for walks and who enjoys the occasional meal out in a nice restaurant or country pub. I'm not looking for a toyboy or a sugar daddy. I don't need a knight in shining armour to come and sweep me off my feet and buy me anything my heart desires. I just need a normal guy, ideally someone who lives around here and has had a similar upbringing to me.

But will I find it?

As I begin my search and start browsing through the first batch of available options, I almost feel embarrassed, like I'm browsing an aisle at the supermarket for tinned goods and not actually picking a real human being to potentially have a future interaction with. Is this really how the kids do dating these days? I mean, sure, it seems easy, just swiping my thumb and pushing the odd button, but it's a little impersonal, isn't it?

I'm almost thinking this is a waste of time as I scroll through a catalogue of headshots of various men alongside short bios in which they list their age, location and hobbies. But then I see a profile that is appealing to me and stop to look at it a little more.

His name is John, he's 51, and he lives locally. He also enjoys walks in the countryside, watching TV and spending time with family and friends. Clicking on the photo of him, the one in which he looks handsome with his silver hair, tanned skin and smart clothing, I am able to learn a little more about him, which is how I read that he has two daughters of his own from his first marriage. A parent to a girl – we have that in common. We also have in common the fact that we have lost our partners because he states that he is a widower.

This guy looks and sounds good and while he obviously comes with a bit of baggage, I have to accept that any man in the age bracket I am searching in will surely come with a bit of a history. But I have my own history too, as does everybody else, and that's just life, so I shouldn't let that put me off clicking the button that will tell John that I am interested in sharing a few messages with him and seeing where it might lead.

So that's what I do, and just like that, I'm back in the game.

Will I meet the perfect guy on here?

Unlikely, but possibly.

I just want a little slice of happiness.

I just want what my daughter has.

8

ELLIE

I just want my husband to get off his phone and pay me a little bit more attention.

Considering we've only just got married and this is technically our honeymoon period before we return to our normal lives, I don't think that's too much to ask, though I won't be pushy because there's no way I'm starting my time as a wife by nagging the man I have just wedded. Besides, it's hard to stay mad at him when I only have to look down at the fourth finger on my left hand and see the ring he bought me when he proposed to me, that question being the thing that led to us being here, in Turkey, smiling for the camera and looking forward to a lifetime of happiness together.

At some point when I get home, I'll have to get around to legally changing my surname so that it matches my husband's.

Ellie Beaumont.

That has a nice ring to it.

As I see Mr Beaumont on the other side of the pool, talking into his mobile phone once again, I recline on my sun lounger and think about how there are much worse ways to spend a Monday afternoon. I'm currently basking in thirty-degree heat with a cold cocktail and a good paperback book for company, and I wouldn't want to be anywhere else. I certainly wouldn't want to be at home because, as Mum just told me in her most recent text message, it's raining there.

Urgh.

As Kyle continues to chatter away, out of earshot but within my sight, I pick up my drink and take a sip before looking around at some of the other people sharing this pool with me and my man. There are a few other couples - some close to our age, others much older - but one thing there is no sign of is children. That's because this is an adults-only hotel, meaning little ones are barred, and that means it's very quiet here. Almost too quiet, if you ask me, because I've never been someone who disliked the sound of children laughing and splashing around in a pool, so I wouldn't have minded if there were a few cute kids around here. But it was Kyle's idea to stay here, and he said it would be more relaxing if the hotel wasn't full of screaming children and their stressed-out parents.

I guess he is right, though I did cheekily remind him that it wouldn't be too long before we were joining the world of those stressed-out parents, chasing after our noisy son or daughter because while we're not in any rush, we have discussed the prospect of parenthood, and it's something both of us are keen to experience. But not yet. We've just married, and we should enjoy each other's company for a while before we start trying to add somebody else to the equation. That's why this adult-only place was probably a good idea, and it's certainly easy to relax here as I put my cocktail down and pick up my book. But just before I start turning the pages on it again to find out how the unpredictable story ends, I glance once more at Kyle and see that he is still on his phone. He's working, so it's not as if he has abandoned me for a frivolous chat with a friend whom he could easily talk to some other time. That at least makes me sympathetic to him because I'm sure that, like me, he'd rather be lounging by this pool than handling boring business. Then again, it is the business he owns, so I guess it's not boring to him, and it probably shouldn't be boring to me for much longer because I might end up working for my husband one day.

I was very impressed when, after meeting Kyle and starting to get to know him better, he told me that he ran his own successful company. Basically, he's a trader of goods, although he never actually handles any of the things he buys or sells, simply negotiating their movement as they get shipped to various places all around the world. According to Kyle, actually having a warehouse full of physical stock is not only expensive but unnecessary in this online age, and the best thing to do is to keep things moving, which is exactly what he does and is why he can run his entire business operation with just his phone and his laptop. A few quick calls or a couple of emails is all it takes for him to complete yet another transaction, meaning he's either buying or selling something that he will then make a profit on before he repeats the whole process again. He calls it logistics and sees himself as an international businessman; I call him a trader and see him as an entrepreneur, while Mum calls it shipping and refers to Kyle as a bit of a 'wheeler dealer'. But whatever the name for it is, there is no denying that he is good at it and is turning over a nice profit, hence why he is able to afford such a nice house back in England that I am very grateful to now be able to call my home too.

I moved in with Kyle only a couple of months after we started dating, eagerly accepting his invitation to move in with him at his place and not just because it was much better than the place I was currently living in. I was just glad because our relationship really seemed to be going somewhere, which is why I left the small flat I had been renting and joined him in the three-bedroom house he told me he purchased a couple of years ago at a great price. His house seemed far too big for just him, but I was more than happy to fill it, and I'll be more than happy to keep living there even when we do have one or two kids because it's certainly big enough. The garden has ample space for a swing set and for playing games of hide and seek and football, and the kitchen table can seat plenty of people around it, making me dream of hosting family Christmas meals in the future.

Kyle's place, or *our place* as I need to start remembering to refer to it as, is so nice that I almost miss it as I sit here around 2,000 miles away from it.

Almost.

It really is nice here, and I do wish we were staying for longer or having our proper honeymoon like Kyle and I have talked about. We plan to go to the Maldives, and it would have been brilliant if we had flown straight there after our wedding. But that trip is delayed and will have to be booked at some point in the future because Kyle needs to be back home tomorrow so he can sort a few things out at the bank regarding his business. He wasn't particularly happy about it, and neither was I, but that's just life, and we can hardly complain considering the brilliant wedding we've just had. However, Kyle suggested we go home sooner, almost immediately after our big day, so he could sort out what he needed to back in England, but I insisted we have at least a couple of days to ourselves before returning. We'll never be in this period of time again, where we're both still basking in the happiness we got from saying our nuptials to one another, so I felt we had to do something to mark it. That's why we're here in this hotel, and Kyle has slowly come around to my way of thinking, though he was a little grumpy at first. That's my husband, a bit of a workaholic, and he's proving it again now because he's still on his phone instead of lying on this lounger next to me. But at least he is ambitious and driven, which is a little more than could be said for me because I've certainly never been one to work too hard and neglect the more fun parts of life.

While I've come a long way from the days when I used to live at home with my mum and work part-time in a restaurant, a job I hated and gladly quit in the end, I have hardly ascended the career ladder and made my own success story in the world of business. I've tried my hand in various workplaces over the past five years since all my drama with Daryl, from offices to call centres, but have never really found something I enjoyed. I'm currently employed as an admin assistant for a fish food company, which is hardly what I would call living the dream, but I guess that's always been my problem.

I have never quite known exactly what my dream is.

However, once Kyle came into my life then I started to figure it out. I don't care about having some high-powered job or earning lots of money, and I certainly don't want to be somebody's boss one day. What I want is to have a home full of love, a partner I can grow old with, a real companion in life, and that is what I now have. Maybe that's why I'm quite liking the idea that one day soon, I can quit my job and be more of a housewife. That would suit me just fine.

I guess a big part of the reason why I value having a loving partner in my life is because I have seen the devastating impact of what losing one can do to a person and their wider family. Seeing Dad go was devastating for me but even harder on Mum, and I know it's not been easy for her to have to do so much on her own, including looking after me. I cringe when I think how hard I used to make things for her back when I was living at home in my early twenties, staying in my room, arguing with her if she ever came in and generally being a big waste of space and adding to her woes rather than making her life more pleasurable. I haven't been the easiest daughter, and that's not even taking into account what happened with my American boyfriend and the total mess that was.

I promised myself I wouldn't think about Daryl anymore, not now I've moved on and found a proper man, one who treats me well and is not a danger to me or others. However, as it has been every day over these last five years since Mum killed Daryl, I find it impossible not to get flashbacks to that terrible time. The nightmares that haunted me in the first year or so after my ordeal have stopped, thankfully, but the memory remains, and it's hard not to go back to that dark time in my mind every now and again. Sometimes, I think about what a fool I was to fall for somebody who was such a good liar, while at other times I feel panicked because I really did come close to not surviving him. That scares me, not just because of the fact that I could easily be dead now, but because if I was, Mum would have lost me as well as her husband.

How could she have ever coped after that? I dread to think what her life would have become if she had been forced to bury her child only a few years after she had buried her husband. Thank God she never had to go through that, and we were able to come out on top, defeating Daryl and his dad.

As far as I know, Harvey is still in prison, though his sentence must be ending soon.

I wonder what he'll do when he gets out.

Unlike Mum, he has to live without his child.

Do I feel sorry for him?

No.

That's just the price he has to pay for raising a killer.

9

HARVEY

Despite packing my bag and heading to the airport two days ago with the intention of boarding the first flight to Amsterdam, a country I can enter easily despite my criminal record, I am still in the US. That's because there were no flights to the Dutch capital with spare seats when I first tried to get there, nor were there any spares on any of the other flights to various cities in the Netherlands. Instead of being on the move quickly, like I wanted to be, I was told by a bored-looking clerk at the check-in desk that the first available flight I could purchase a ticket for would be in over forty-eight hours' time. I expressed my frustration, but there was little I could do, and not wanting to cause a scene and draw the attention of any of the police officers on patrol at LAX, I just bought my ticket and then said I'd be back when it was time for my flight. After that, I returned home, and I've been here ever since, impatiently biding my time until I can start churning through the air miles between me and the people I ultimately want to pay a visit to in England. But I have hardly been idle in that time and have been kept busy, though I can't say much of it has been fun for me.

One of the benefits of catching a quick flight out of LA would have been not having to see Clara again and keep pretending like we were going to have a long and happy future together as a couple. However, because I've been stuck here for a couple of days longer than I wanted to be, I have had to see her again. She came to my place yesterday, aware of the address because it got leaked online back when mine and Daryl's story was in the news and the trolls on social media were talking about burning the place to the ground. Thankfully, nobody actually did that, but it did mean an awful lot of people knew where I lived. At least only Clara has turned up at my front door so far. Better her than some vigilante wanting to carry out his own form of justice for the crimes my son and I partook in. Even worse than that, I have always worried about somebody with a connection to Aubree Parker, the young woman my son murdered, coming to my house to speak to me. It's not that I fear them attacking me, as such, it's more that I don't particularly want to hear them tell their story about how the whole case affected them because while I feel sorry for them, talking about it won't change what has already happened. As it is, no one from that woman's family has been to see me, and I imagine they have tried to move on as best they can.

With Clara calling by yesterday, I had to go through the motions and pretend like I was serious about us being a real couple once again. That meant listening to her as she talked about what life would be like when we lived together, as well as falling into bed with her again to keep up appearances. Okay, so that part wasn't the biggest hardship ever, but I'd have much rather preferred to have been on the other side of the Atlantic Ocean than stuck in LA, though at least the weather has improved, and it's back to clear blue skies and warm temperatures.

Having successfully kept Clara under my spell for another day, I bid her farewell as she left my house yesterday. But it wasn't long after Clara had come to see me that I had another visitor at my door, and this time, it was a Probation Officer who had come to talk to me and offer advice about the best way for me to reintegrate myself back into society. Through gritted teeth, I had to sit with him and say that I was very much looking forward to becoming a positive and productive member of the community again now that my problematic past was behind me, and the officer had lots of ideas about how I could do just that, ideas that I had no real interest in hearing. It was suggested that I do some volunteer work as a way to give back to the city but also as a thing that would be good for my soul, considering my tainted past. I was also advised of ways to get back into work, and that was encouraged not just because everybody needs to make money somehow, but because it would reduce the time I had available to sit around and think about everything that had happened in the past.

"The future is under your control" was the mantra that the officer kept espousing, and while I agreed with it in general, the way I planned to put it into action in my life greatly differed from what the officer had in mind. While they were surely thinking about me turning my life around and making a success of myself after a period behind bars, I was simply thinking about killing Dawn and Ellie.

The future is under my control.

I liked that idea very much, particularly when it came to thoughts of my revenge.

It was hardly fun, but I eventually dealt with the probation officer, and once they had left, all I had to do was get through one more night before I could return to LAX and finally board a flight. That night was accompanied by little sleep, though it had less to do with me being eager to fly and more to do with the fact that I spent an awfully long time trawling through the multitude of articles that had been written online about my son and me since I had been in prison.

There were also more than a few about Dawn and Ellie too.

The journalists who had penned the pieces clearly had an agenda and made sure to report on Daryl and me as the villains, while the mother and daughter in England were the heroes of the story, depicted as the brave women who had battled against the odds and defeated their devious and deadly American counterparts. It was no wonder I struggled to sleep as I read article after article about how bad I was as a father or about how despicable my son was, before reading about how strong Dawn was to save her daughter and how perfect Ellie was before my son entered her life. Of course, some of it was true but so much of it was embellished and some of it was downright lies. Dawn and Ellie aren't the perfect people they have been made out to be in the articles, and I got the sense their relationship was strained when they came to stay with us. But that doesn't make for as good a story as writing that they were inseparable and lived for each other because that only makes what ended up happening seem even more wonderful.

As for lies about me and Daryl, they made out like my son had been a problem child and was well known for causing trouble throughout his school life, which was nonsense. I have also been portrayed as a controlling, coercive father who ruled with an iron fist, which, again, couldn't be further from the truth. The more I read, the more I felt like there weren't many journalists out there who would know what the real truth was if it came along and slapped them in the face, but in a way, that also helped me. They haven't got a clue - just making assumptions and forming generic opinions - no different to Dawn or Ellie, or the police, for that matter.

Nobody really knows who I am and what makes me tick.

That will work in my favour very shortly.

However, reading all the articles wasn't a total waste of my time because in amongst all the click-bait headlines there were a few recent stories which allowed me to find out what that mother and daughter were up to these days. There was a photo of Dawn shopping at her local supermarket, as if that constitutes news, though the editor who commissioned the story obviously thought it did, going with the headline *'Five Years Since Saving Her Daughter – Life Goes On For Hero Mum.'*

There was also a photo of Ellie in the story, showing her walking along the high street in her hometown carrying a couple of shopping bags and, again, the angle of the news story seemed to be that after all the drama that they had endured before, normality had resumed, and they had put the past behind them.

Seeing those photos only made me more determined to remind Dawn and Ellie that there is no such thing as normality anymore, not after they killed my son, and it galls me that they are just going about their lives, shopping and doing everyday chores without a care in the world.

It feels like it's time to make the headlines a little juicier.

I might get my wish very soon because, as of right now, I am in the taxi to LAX, and unlike last time I went there, I already have a plane ticket booked. That's why, when I enter the airport, I am quickly able to check-in my luggage before I am handed my boarding pass, and then all I need to do is get through the security checks. I'm hoping there will be no issue as I place the items in my pockets into the tray and then pass through the body scanner, but with a criminal record, my paranoia is heightened slightly. But it's not as if I'm on a terrorist watchlist, so even with my history, I make it through without any issue, and now the only thing stopping me from boarding my flight is the fact I have a couple of hours to kill until the gate opens.

I while away that time by getting something to eat and browsing a few of the duty-free shops, but eventually, I start to grow more impatient and go and stand in front of the large electronic Departures screen that hangs above the busy terminal I'm standing in. My eyes scan the array of flights that are due to leave LAX over the next several hours, many of them to exotic locations that would make a great place to go for a holiday.

It doesn't take me long to find the destination I am searching for, and I see Amsterdam in bright yellow letters. I also see the gate number flashing beside it, and that tells me where I can go to board the plane.

This is it; I'm finally on my way.

Ten hours in the sky to get me closer to Dawn and Ellie.

Next stop - Europe.

10

DAWN

I squint my eyes at the large Arrivals screen above me while trying not to get bumped and barged into by all the passengers who are rushing around this busy section of the airport. I'm looking for Ellie's flight from Turkey so I can make sure it has landed on time, and it's a relief when I see that it has, mainly because it means I won't have to return to my car and put more hours on the parking meter.

While Kyle and Ellie messaged to let me know that they were more than happy to get a taxi home after returning from their trip, I told them that I would collect them, though not just because I wanted to do something nice for them and save them a few pounds on a fare. It's because I'm super excited to see them and hear about their last few days, as well as talk about the wedding itself and relive that wonderful day that simply went too fast when it was actually happening.

Seeing that my daughter's flight has landed, I go to join the dozens of people who are already in position at the Arrivals gate to collect their loved ones after they have touched down, and while space is at a premium, I manage to get myself into a decent position where I think Ellie or Kyle should be able to spot me when they walk through here soon.

The electronic doors that allow passengers to walk out to us keep sliding open and shut, and I see a lot of people appearing, wheeling suitcases behind them and flashing big grins when they see their family members or friends waiting for them, proving what a great time they must have had on whatever trip they have just undertaken. I'm expecting to see big smiles on the faces of Ellie and Kyle when they emerge any second too, because they will still surely be basking in that wonderful glow that every couple has when they have only recently married and life still seems like one big exciting adventure to be undertaken together. I remember that feeling with Sean, and they might as well enjoy it while it lasts because, unfortunately, real life soon rears its ugly head again, and before a married couple knows it, they are brought back down to reality with bills that are due to pay, house chores that need to be completed and a realisation that everyday life is not quite as enthralling as the wedding day itself was.

The doors slide open and shut four more times before I catch a glimpse of the two people I am here to meet, but when I see them, they are not looking as happy as I would have expected them to be. Kyle seems a little grumpy and, in a rush, marching ahead of Ellie, who is walking behind him with her head bowed, and while she has a bit of a suntan from her time in Turkey, she isn't exactly glowing as radiantly as a new wife should be.

Oh no. I hope they've not had their first argument as a married couple. If so, this car journey home could be a bit of an awkward one.

'Hey, guys! Over here!' I cry, waving to the newlyweds to get their attention so they can spot me in the crowd, and when Ellie sees me, she nudges Kyle and points me out to him.

He doesn't exactly look thrilled to see me but forces a polite smile onto his face, but I just put that down to the fact that after a long journey, mothers-in-law aren't always at the top of the list for a guy to be faced with. I suspect he and Ellie both just want to get home and relax after spending several hours travelling, so I will aim to make this last part of their journey as painless as possible for them both.

'Hi, guys. Welcome back!' I say, hugging Ellie while Kyle stands by a little awkwardly before I offer him a hug too. 'Did you have a good flight?'

'Yeah, it was alright,' Kyle says, looking a little tired.

'Thanks for picking us up, Mum. You didn't have to,' Ellie says, but I dismiss that before offering to help carry some of their luggage.

Kyle says he can manage, but Ellie gladly hands me one of the three bags she is hauling around with her, and then the three of us make our way out of the airport and into the car park where I left my vehicle. As we go, I notice that Ellie and Kyle aren't chatting much with each other, but I make up for it, filling the silence by asking them how their brief honeymoon was after the wedding.

'It was lovely. The pool was nice, wasn't it?' Ellie says to Kyle, and he nods his head.

'Yeah, great,' he replies as he puts his suitcase into the back of my car, but his answer seems a little half-hearted. I wonder if he is just suffering from the dreaded post-holiday blues. Nobody likes getting home after a wonderful time abroad, so maybe that's simply the reason he's not quite in top form. I suppose he'd rather still be sitting by that pool than back here beneath this ashen sky, preparing to get into his mother-in-law's car before getting ready to go back to work tomorrow. At least I presume he is back at work, but that thought gives me something else to ask him.

'Have you got any more time off or are you back to the daily grind?' I ask Kyle.

'Yeah, back to work for me now,' he says before Ellie cuts in.

'Back to work? You never really stopped while we were away.'

I get the hint that this is the reason for the slight frostiness between the new couple, so I decide to change the subject quickly.

'Well, let's get going,' I say, opening the car doors so my passengers can get in. 'I'm sure you are eager to get back home and unpack.'

With that, I jump into the driver's seat and then I'm off, navigating my way out of this multi-storey car park that occasionally makes me feel like I need a map to figure my way around it. I'm relieved once we're on the main road, and as I drive in the direction of Ellie and Kyle's place, I must admit, I am quite looking forward to being in their house again. *It is lovely.* Technically, it's still more Kyle's place than Ellie's because he had it before they were married, so it's all in his name. But my daughter says the plan is for them to stay there, and I'm sure they'll get around to sorting out whatever paperwork needs to be done so that they can both be joint owners of the property. I know Ellie is already contributing her share of the bills for the place, although quite how long that will last is unclear because she has already told me that she quite likes the idea of quitting her job and being a lady of leisure.

Wouldn't we all, hey?

But if that's what my daughter does, then I won't be jealous in the slightest. I'd much rather she have that kind of lifestyle than spend her life doing what her mother has done, which is work constantly in a low-paying job for little reward. I never had a choice but if Ellie does, she should take the opportunity while she can.

Thankfully, Ellie and Kyle are a little chattier as we drive on, and by the time we reach the house, I feel like they aren't really mad at each other, just weary from their trip. That's why I make sure to tell them that I won't stay for long, simply helping them get their bags inside before leaving them to it.

'No, stay for a cup of tea, Mum,' Ellie says, and if the invite is there, I won't refuse it because I would like a catch-up with my girl, so I agree to stay for a little while.

After we have got the bags inside, Kyle thanks me for helping before saying he has a couple of calls to make and will go upstairs to do them. Ellie just rolls her eyes at that, but in a jokey way, and as he leaves us, she enters the kitchen to put the kettle on. I go to follow her but just before I do, I notice there are a few letters lying on the doormat, post that was pushed through the letterbox while the occupants were away. Wanting to continue being helpful, I pick them up and put them on the side table at the bottom of the stairs. But as I do, I notice the name on one of the envelopes.

Julia Beaumont.

Hmmm, that's weird. This woman has the same surname as Kyle and the same surname that Ellie will soon be assuming once she has legally applied to have it changed from her maiden one.

Who is this woman? I think for a moment but don't recall ever hearing about a Julia from either Kyle or Ellie. That means it can't be a sibling or some other family relative of his, right? I mean, he would have mentioned her, surely, and she would have been at the wedding. But Kyle's an only child, so it's definitely not a sister, and his mum has passed away. So who could it be?

I think about going into the kitchen and asking Ellie, although that seems a little nosey of me, so maybe not. But it turns out that I don't have to do that because a second later, Kyle comes back downstairs.

'I need my phone charger,' he says, before unzipping one of the bags that litter the hallway and going in search of it.

This seems like a good opportunity to casually mention the name I'm having trouble placing, seeing as I'm standing here with the envelope in my hand, so I go for it while Ellie is out of earshot.

'There was some mail on the doormat, so I've picked it up for you,' I say, and Kyle says thanks, though he looks far more interested in finding his charger so he can get on with making his calls.

Here goes nothing.

'Sorry. I couldn't help but notice there is some mail addressed to a Julia Beaumont. Is that a family member of yours?'

I deliberately allow my sentence to trail off, inviting Kyle to fill the space with his answer, but he's not exactly quick to do so. He does, however, stop rummaging in his bag for his charger and look up at me.

'Oh, erm, can I see it?' he asks, and I hand him the envelope in question.

'Sorry, I don't mean to pry or anything. I just saw it when I picked it up,' I say in my defence in case Kyle is going to accuse me of being nosey. But he doesn't do that.

'No, it's okay. Don't worry about it. This is just for the person who used to live here before me.'

'Julia lived here before you?'

'That's right.'

'Oh, I see. She had the same surname as you?'

'Yeah, a bit of a coincidence there. I'll have to return this to the post office at some point.'

Kyle shrugs before stuffing the letter into his pocket and then going back to looking for his charger. But I watch him for a moment, trying to figure out why I feel a little uneasy.

Is it really a coincidence that the previous owner of this house had the same surname as my daughter's husband?

Or has he just told me a lie?

If so, why?

11

DAWN

I didn't press Kyle any further about the name on the letter, nor did I mention it to Ellie when I had a cup of tea with her shortly after I saw it. I decided to park any doubts I had about what Kyle said and focus on listening to my daughter excitedly go over her wedding day in great detail, enlightening me on any parts of it I missed while I was elsewhere in the venue talking to other people. It was lovely to hear how much of a good time Ellie had during her big day, as well as hear all about the couple of days she stayed in Turkey with only Kyle for company. As I suspected, there had been a little bit of an issue between them, and it was caused by Kyle taking several work calls during the break when Ellie would have preferred he spent all that time with her. But she wasn't too upset about it, aware that he enjoys his job and is doing well at it, and I made sure to gently remind her that even though he can be busy, everything he is doing is not just for him but her now as well.

We finished our drinks, and then I decided to give the couple some space, leaving and telling them that I would see them soon. But as I made my way home, the name on the envelope did return to my mind a few times, even though I tried my best to forget about it.

The thing is, I'm very conscious of the fact that it would be very easy for me to never trust any of Ellie's partners again after what happened previously with Daryl. But I refuse to let myself succumb to being paranoid and untrusting of any of her relationships, going forward, just because of one bad experience. Besides, if I lived like that, it's almost like Daryl has won, even though he's gone. There's also the fact that if Ellie can find it within herself to trust another man again, I should be able to do it, which is why I am really trying my hardest to trust Kyle when he told me that woman with the same surname as him was just a previous occupant at the house and nothing more.

Forget about it, Dawn. Ellie is happy now. Kyle is a good man.

There's nothing to worry about there.

While that might be easier said than done, I'm fortunate that I have something planned tonight that will definitely take my mind off things, for a couple of hours at least. That's because I'm going on a date, and it will be the first date I've been on in a very long time.

Amazingly, despite not expecting much, the man I indicated a bit of interest in on the app a short time ago indicated his interest in me too, and that was how we started messaging each other. John, the silver-haired and handsome male who caught my eye when I was browsing through the list of available men, said that he'd love to go for a drink with me, and when I replied saying I'd be interested in such a thing, a date was set.

And that date is tonight.

No sooner have I got back from Ellie's place then I am rushing around my own house trying to get ready in time. I shower first before taking an awfully long time to settle on an outfit to wear. It's only a drink that we're going for, but the way I peruse the options in the wardrobe, it's as if I'm going for dinner with the King of England. But after eventually settling on an outfit that is sophisticated but not too dour, because I still want to seem fun, I can get on with the mammoth task of applying make-up and sorting my hair out.

It feels strange to be sitting at the dressing table in my spare bedroom and applying mascara and blusher because I genuinely cannot remember the last time I did this at home. Sure, I beautified myself for the wedding in Turkey recently, but that was a one-off event. It has been a very, very long time since I put this much effort into my appearance on a regular day in my ordinary life. But the more make-up I apply, the better I start to feel about myself, and I feel even happier when I've treated myself to a glass of wine from the fridge downstairs. I just need one drink to take the edge off my nerves, and I wonder if John is doing the same thing before he leaves his place to meet me.

We're set to liaise at a wine bar on the high street, a venue that John selected, though it is one I know well because I've frequented it before with my friends. Oh God, I hope neither Maggie nor Tanya are going to be in there tonight because if they are then they will see me out with a new man, and they will begin gossiping immediately. They will want to know who he is and what is going on and, most of all, why I have kept quiet about it to them. But the truth is, I've kept it quiet from everyone, Ellie included, because I have no idea if this is the start of anything or if it will just be one big waste of time.

I won't mention entering the world of dating again until I know there is some substance to it. No point getting Maggie and Tanya all excited for me yet, nor is there any point risking Ellie being a little upset that her mum is moving on from her father. But I'm sure Ellie will understand if there does come a time when I explain to her that I have started seeing a new man, though I won't make that a conversation topic until I am absolutely certain it is worth me doing so and so far, it's not.

John could turn out to be a weirdo or a bore or just not a very nice guy.

I hope not, but who knows?

There's only one way to find out.

After ordering my taxi and spending a final few minutes checking on my appearance in the hallway mirror, I exit my house and get into the back of the vehicle that has arrived to deliver me to the wine bar. I hope John is going to be on time because that wouldn't be good if he was already giving me reasons to doubt his suitability for me, but it's a relief when I enter the bar and see him wave to me from a table in the corner.

I recognise him because he clearly was honest about his appearance on the dating app, and he looks exactly like the photo he used on there. He obviously feels the same way about me because he didn't hesitate to spot me when I walked in, and as I reach him, the pair of us don't quite seem to know how to greet the other.

A hug? A handshake? A kiss on the cheek or just a friendly smile and a hello?

In the end, we make a bit of a mess of it and do some sort of awkward combination of all of the above before taking our seats. Then we end up bumping hands as we both reach for the drinks menu at the same time.

This has started well.

Giggling nervously, we both admit to not having done this sort of thing for a long time, and that seems to allow us both to relax. Then, once our drinks are ordered, we start to get to know each other a little more than our heavily edited dating profiles allow and discuss the parts of town we come from, how long we have lived here and how things have changed over the years. Once our drinks have been delivered to our table, we start to get a little more personal.

'I have one daughter, Ellie,' I say proudly. 'She just got married in Turkey.'

'How wonderful! I thought you had a bit of a suntan,' John says with a big smile, and I guess it's a good thing that he thinks I have a healthy complexion.

'I didn't get much sun because I wasn't out there for long, but it was a great occasion, and my daughter was very happy.'

'Do you get on well with your son-in-law?'

'Yes, I'd say so. He's a lovely guy,' I reply. 'Successful too. He runs his own business.'

'Wow, it sounds like your daughter has really landed on her feet with him.'

'I'd say he's landed on his feet with her too.'

'Of course. Well, how about a toast? To your daughter and her husband. I wish them all the very best.'

That's a nice gesture from John, so I thank him as we clink glasses before he tells me all about his daughters, although the news there isn't quite as uplifting because one of them is currently going through a divorce.

'Oh, that's a shame. I'm sorry,' I say, whilst hoping Ellie never has to deal with anything like that, though if she ever did, I would be right by her side to help her.

As I watch John light up as he talks about his daughters and their hobbies, I think about what a lovely man he is and how this date is going far better than I expected. That's why, when he has finished his latest story, I suggest we get another drink. But just before we do, John has something else to say.

'I'm sorry, but it's been bugging me ever since we sat down together. I feel like I recognise you from somewhere.'

Oh no. There it is. The reference to the thing I have been dreading. He must have seen my photo in the news. That's it, isn't it? If so, what is he going to do?

'Erm,' I say, stalling for time before I have an idea. 'I work in a supermarket. The big one on Reynolds Street.'

I'm hoping I can deflect away from where he has probably seen me, which is in the news, and make him think he might have seen me at my workplace. It's not that I know I could keep my past secret forever if things develop between us, but I don't want it to be discussed tonight, on our first date, especially as it has been going so well thus far.

'Oh, that might be it,' John says, much to my relief. 'I have shopped in there a few times, so I must have seen you in the aisles.'

'Yeah, possibly,' I say before catching the attention of the waitress and hoping another drinks order will make John forget that about me seeming familiar. It appears to do the trick because after ordering our drinks, John changes the subject, and we start discussing our own hobbies. It turns out that we are compatible in terms of our movie choices, which bodes well for a potential cinema date in the future, and the more I'm here enjoying myself, the more I realise my friends were right all along. I did need to put myself out there and try and move on from Sean because there is plenty of happiness to be found if I would only go looking for it.

And then that happiness fades away almost as quickly as I found it.

It happens when I'm on my way back from the bathroom after briefly excusing myself from our table, and as I return to my seat, I catch a glimpse at what John has been looking at on his phone while I've been gone. I see a photo of me and Ellie beside one of Daryl, and that tells me that John realised he recognised me from the news and not the supermarket like I pretended was the case.

Not aware that I've caught him reading up about me online, John quickly puts his phone back in his pocket when he sees I have come back to the table, and as I retake my seat, I decide to broach the difficult subject because it would be better for me to explain it to him than some journalist who embellished half the story.

But I don't get the chance to do that because John suddenly tells me that something has happened with a friend and he needs to leave, and he stands up quickly before throwing down a few £10 notes on the table to cover the drinks we have had and the ones that are about to come.

'Do you want to do this again?' I ask him before he can rush away, but he just tells me that he'll be in touch, and then he is gone, practically running out of the door as he goes.

As the waitress reappears with the two drinks I ordered, I realise that my date isn't coming back, and I'm left here alone. I also realise that just like I thought, my past might work against me when it comes to finding a new man.

Can I blame them?

Who wants to date a killer?

Sure, I was only defending my daughter but there's baggage and then there's the baggage that I come with.

John, most likely, just wants a normal woman he can introduce to his family and friends.

But I'm not normal, not after what I did, and I guess I never will be.

Nobody who lived through that whole sorry experience will ever be the same again.

12

HARVEY

Life usually seems calmer at 38,000ft, as if the problems on the ground seem insignificant when high up above them. But sometimes, a problem can be so big that no amount of distance or perspective can make it appear smaller, and that is how I feel as the plane I am seated in hurtles me towards Europe. It's a ten-hour flight from LA to Amsterdam, and then God knows how many hours of travel time after that if I am to make it into England as discreetly as possible. That's a long time for me to sit and ponder what I am going to do to Dawn and Ellie when I finally see them again, which is why I'm trying to make my journey as comfortable as I can.

'One more, please,' I say to the male member of the cabin crew who has just passed down the aisle to see if anybody in this section of the aircraft would like another drink.

No sooner have I indicated to him that I would then he is quickly getting to work fixing me another whiskey, and while this beverage out of a can won't taste as good as if it was poured straight from a bottle, it's better than nothing. I can't fly all this way and be totally sober, not with so much to sit here and think about as I'm strapped into my seat high above the Atlantic Ocean. Besides, a little alcohol should also help me drift off to sleep at some point during the flight, which would be a blessing because I'm not much of a movie guy, so I'm struggling with the in-flight entertainment options.

However, one form of entertainment on this journey so far has come in the form of me trying to figure out how many people on this plane might recognise me and if so, if any of them are going to do anything about it.

I am wearing an LA Dodgers baseball cap to try and disguise myself as best I can, and it seemed to work pretty well as I made my way through the crowded airport earlier. I didn't attract any glances, or at least I didn't think I did, which was important because in this day and age, everybody has a phone, meaning everybody can be a journalist.

I didn't want somebody recognising me as the father of a killer and mentioning it on social media and then that news making its way to the phones of an actual journalist who has the power to spread that message far and wide. I want to keep my name out of the headlines, at least until I've completed my revenge, so not being recognised is important to me. I don't need people speculating about where I might be going or even just having people talk about me being released because so far, that bit of news has gone under the radar, which is a little surprising to me, if I'm honest. I thought there might have been a journalist or two waiting outside the prison when I was let go, to film footage of the first few moments of my freedom. I definitely expected there to be a few camera crews coming to my home once one of my neighbours spotted me and started to spread the word that I was back. But that's not happened. Maybe it's because five years have passed, and everyone has moved on with their lives. There must certainly have been plenty of other crimes committed in that time for people to grow bored of me and my story.

That's a good thing because I want everyone to be bored of me.

I want to be forgotten.

Right up until the moment when I am not.

'Vacation or business?'

The sudden question from the female passenger sitting beside me presents me with an interesting dilemma. Shall I be honest with her or not?

'A bit of both,' I say, and to me, that is actually the most truthful answer. I can't say that it's not business that is seeing me fly all this way, but on the other hand, I can't pretend like it's not something I don't want to do either. Killing Dawn and Ellie will feel like conducting business and taking a holiday, both at the same time.

'Interesting,' the woman replies. 'Just business for me.'

'What is it you do for work?' I ask her, willing to make conversation for two reasons. One, to pass the time, and two, because this person clearly has no idea that I am infamous in LA, otherwise she wouldn't be so friendly with me now.

'I'm a doctor specialising in psychology. I'll be speaking at a medical conference in Amsterdam in a couple of days.'

'Psychology? I bet that's fascinating.'

'It can be. I guess it depends on the subject.'

'True,' I reply, before waiting for the inevitable question to be returned to me and sure enough, it is.

'And what is it you do?' the doctor asks me with keen interest.

'I'm actually in between jobs at the moment,' I reply calmly, quite liking my answer. 'I've had a long break, but now I'm just starting to get back into things.'

'Things?'

'I can't really talk about it,' I say with a hint of mischief as if I'm some secret agent on a mission that nobody else is qualified to know about. At best, I'm thinking I might pique the interest of the attractive medical professional who is sitting beside me, and we might end up harmlessly flirting for a while. Or, at worst, she'll realise I'm being a bit vague with her and might go back to minding her own business, which would be absolutely fine by me. But then she leans in and what she says stuns me.

'That's understandable,' she tells me in a low voice. 'I mean, if my son was a killer and I'd just gone to prison for trying to cover it up, then I wouldn't want to tell too many people about it either.'

I stare at the doctor and process what she just said, but there's not really too much to think about. She obviously knows exactly who I am and has just called me out on it. So much for my baseball cap helping me keep a low profile.

'Excuse me?' I say, feigning ignorance.

'I know who you are,' she replies calmly. 'Harvey, right? And your son's name was Daryl.'

Yep, she knows who I am, alright.

I'm not quite sure what to say to her, so I stay quiet and allow her to continue.

'So I guess you're out then,' she goes on. 'It's been a few years, hasn't it? Served your sentence, have you? Done your time? Paid the price and now you're all rehabilitated and ready to be a productive member of society again?'

'What is this?'

'Nothing, I'm just saying that you seem to be doing quite well for a man who went to prison for a serious crime. I mean, here you are, jetting off to Amsterdam. Not bad, hey?'

'Doing well? I lost my son and went to prison for five years,' I say, keeping my voice low so none of the other passengers seated around us might hear me because I don't need even more people recognising me and giving me trouble.

'And Aubree Parker's parents lost their daughter, and she's never coming back,' the woman tells me with a menacing look. 'They were innocent, and you and your son hurt them and now what? You think you can just drink whiskey on a plane and go and see another country and everything is alright again because you've served your time? You and your son are a disgrace, and you should still be in prison. But at least he got what he deserved.'

That last line is too much, and I'm just about to raise my voice to this woman, no longer giving a damn about who might overhear us, but the pilot suddenly comes over the intercom to give us an update on the progress of the flight. That's enough of a distraction to make me pause for a moment, and a second later, the woman beside me gets up from her seat and gathers up her few belongings before going to sit in one of the few vacant seats on this flight.

I guess she's had enough of being around me and made her feelings perfectly clear before she left. But so what, because I'd had enough of being around her too. Who did she think she was to judge me and my son? She certainly had no right to say that Daryl got what he deserved. But what was I to expect? I bet that woman has read every single news article written about us, meaning she's been brainwashed into hating us. I have a good mind to get up from my seat and continue our conversation, telling her that she was out of order to talk to me like that, regardless of what I might have done in the past. I'm still a human being, and I'm still a father who lost his child, regardless of the extenuating circumstances there. But I don't bother doing that because I know it's not worth it.

At least she's the only one who has recognised me on this plane. Or maybe she's the only one who has the guts to say how they really feel to me.

Whatever. I'm not going to let it ruin my flight. Like the pilot just said over the intercom, everything is going to plan.

I can only hope that continues all the way up to the moment when I'm standing outside Dawn and Ellie's home with a sharp knife in one hand and a big smile on my face.

13

DAWN

After the disaster of my first date in decades, I'm in no mood to share the details of it with anybody. Not Ellie. Not my friends. Nobody. I just want to forget that it happened, though I know that is unlikely because it's still so fresh in my mind.

It was only two hours ago when John practically ran out of that bar after figuring out I was the poor woman who had made all the headlines in this town five years ago. Clearly not feeling like I was the type of woman he wanted to introduce to his family and friends, he promptly made his exit, leaving me to use the money he had left behind to settle the bill and then make my own way out of that bar. At least he had the decency to pay for our drinks, so I suppose I can't be too mad at him for cutting our date so short. But I am mad because of the way he acted towards me.

He treated me like I was something hot that he had accidentally picked up, and he had to drop me as soon as possible. Or like I was damaged goods that he had inadvertently encountered, and he needed to get away from me as quickly as possible lest he become damaged too. At least that was how it felt as he looked at me with a mixture of pity and shock - pity because I'd obviously been through a lot but shock because he hadn't expected to be the guy who had to deal with it.

So he left.

No matter. I'm better off without him. Things would never have worked out if he was prone to leaving quickly when times were tough. My past is my past, and I can't change it, and if he wasn't man enough to handle it then that's his problem, not mine.

So if it's his problem, why am I the one currently drowning my sorrows at home, feeling incredibly lonely with only a bottle of wine for company?

I should just leave this alcohol alone and go up to bed, especially because it is late, and I have work tomorrow. But for some reason, I'm not quite ready to call it a day yet, and sleep doesn't seem achievable in this state of mind.

Is it because of my failed first date?

Or is it because something else is playing on my mind?

If I'm honest with myself, there is another reason that I'm sitting here and sipping wine, and it's not just because of John. It's because of Kyle, the son-in-law who seemed a little uncomfortable when I asked him about that name on the envelope earlier.

Why is this still bothering me?

Is it because the more I think about it, the more I believe he was lying?

Knowing there is only one way to find out, I put my wine glass down and go and find my laptop. It's lying on my bed where I left it this morning, but rather than get into bed to use it, which would be more sensible given the late hour, I take it back downstairs to where my wine is waiting.

I allow my device to load up while I pour myself another glass, and then, when it's ready, I start conducting a few Google searches. What I am looking for is a website that will tell me the previous owners of a property, and I know such sites exist because my friends have talked about them before when they have been going through their various house moves. I can't think of anything more stressful and annoying than going through a house move, which is why this is the first home I ever bought and it will also be the last. But my friends have moved a few times each, always looking to upscale and add size for their growing families, and that's how I recall hearing them talking about the modern ways in which a person can look into the history of a house they might be interested in.

Back when I bought this place with Sean, there were no websites to go snooping around on. We basically had to trust the estate agent who was showing us around the place and take his word for it that the property was as appealing as it seemed and that there was no horrible history connected to the building that we didn't know about. But these days, a potential buyer can simply type in an address, and everything about the place is listed.

I've just found out how to do it.

Sipping my wine again whilst trying to tell myself that I'm not acting in an extremely paranoid way here, I vow to just make a quick check to see if the person who owned the property before Kyle had the same surname as him. If so, I will stop snooping because he will have been telling me the truth, and there will be nothing more to it.

But what if I find something that contradicts what he said?

Telling myself that won't happen because Kyle is an honest guy and the perfect man for my daughter to have married, I type in his house number and street name before pressing enter. When the page refreshes, I expect to see a chronological history of the property in question, from dates the house was sold to the values each sale had and, most tellingly for me, the surnames of those who purchased them.

As the history is displayed, I see all those things dating back to the 1980s when the house was originally built. However, almost immediately, I see something that troubles me. The name at the top of this list is not Kyle's, which suggests he is not the owner of the home. Also, the name below it, which would be the person he bought the property from, is not the name I saw on that envelope earlier, proving that was a lie as well.

What is going on?

My first thought is that this website must be showing false information, so I go in search of another one, one that might be a more reputable record of historical fact. That leads me to a site in which I have to pay to get full access to property records, but it's only a small fee per month, and I can cancel it as soon as I have what I need, so I enter my card details and start a subscription. Then I conduct the same search I just did on the other website and hope that I will get different results this time.

But I don't.

According to this, the house is not in Kyle's name, as he has led both me and Ellie to believe. It's in the name of an S McGill. Who the hell is that? And as for that mystery woman who had mail sent to the property, there is no mention of her either.

My first thought is to grab my phone and call Ellie to tell her that her husband is lying to us both and something is going on, something that he clearly doesn't want us to know the truth about. But then I see the time and because it's after midnight, I hesitate. My daughter will most likely be asleep now, not just because it's late but because she told me earlier how exhausted she was after the highs of the wedding and the travel time back from Turkey. She needs her rest, and I shouldn't disturb her. Besides, what can we do at this time? Better to leave it until the morning. I can call her before I go to work and ask her to meet me and then, when Kyle is not around her, I can tell her what I have just discovered.

What will she say?

Will she believe me that something might be wrong?

Or will she accuse me of being paranoid and stifling her and her relationships?

I really hope it's not the latter, but it doesn't matter because I have an obligation to tell her what I know, and it's up to her what she does with that information.

Eager to see if I can find anything on the name S McGill and why Kyle might be living in that person's house whilst pretending it is his own, I search on the internet, narrowing it to look for local results, and very quickly, I get the website for a property company in my town and sure enough, S McGill is listed as the owner.

So Kyle's house is owned by this property company?

What does that make him then? Just a tenant?

So why say he owns the place if he is just renting?

Looking at this property company's portfolio, I see that they purchased the home three years ago at auction. Re-checking the website that lists the home's history, I confirm the name of the person who owned it before does not match the name on that envelope I saw, and it doesn't, confirming Kyle's lie to me.

This is a lot to process.

Maybe I've got mixed up somewhere.

Maybe I've just had too much wine.

I think it's time to call it a night.

Closing my laptop screen after spending far longer than I should, staring at it and trying to make sense of why Kyle might lie about his house and who might have lived there before, I head upstairs to bed with my head swimming with questions. But I know I'm not going to get any answers until all my questions are put to Kyle. But first, I need to put them to Ellie so she is fully in the loop before anything else happens. That's why, before turning off my light and trying to get some sleep, I send her a message saying that I need to talk to her and that she is to give me a call as soon as she wakes up in the morning, no matter how early it is.

She doesn't reply, so she must be asleep.

That's okay.
She's at peace.
I'll let her enjoy that for now.
Soon, she'll be just as worried as I am.

14

ELLIE

There's never more of a reality check for a person than the morning they wake up after several days off to the sound of their alarm clock and the knowledge that they have to go back to work now. That's what I'm currently experiencing as I reach out and turn off my alarm before wearily rubbing my eyes and wondering if the happiness I experienced over the past few days was reality or just some sort of dream. But I get my answer when I look at the other half of the bed and see the handsome man lying beside me because that tells me that it was not a dream at all.

'Good morning, hubby,' I say, the fun of getting to say a sentence like that almost making up for the fact that I have to get up and start my commute to work shortly.

'Good morning, wifey,' Kyle replies with a grin, and the two of us kiss before I lament the fact that we can't just stay in bed together all day and do something more fun than work. I know Kyle has his own work to do because he is already pushing himself up off the mattress and going in search of some clothes, clearly a little more eager to begin his day than I am. If it was up to me, I'd never work again, and as I watch my man making his way to the bathroom, I decide this is a good moment right here to mention that.

'Hurry up and make all your millions so I can retire,' I say, joking, of course, but not completely.

I expect Kyle to make a joke back or perhaps show some bravado in terms of his business acumen and tell me that he is working on some seven-figure deal that will be set to change both our lives very soon. But he doesn't do either of those things. Instead, I just sense that he is troubled by something, and even after he has gone into the bathroom and closed the door, I am worrying that something is on his mind.

I decide to stop being lazy and get out of bed so I can go and check on him, but just before I do that, I notice I have a message on my phone from Mum. She sent it at 1 AM, which is an unusual time for anybody to be messaging me, let alone my mother, who surely should have been asleep at that late hour. She didn't have a night shift at the supermarket last night, as far as I can recall, so what was she doing texting me?

'Call me when you wake up. I'm sure it's nothing to worry about, but we need to talk about something' the message reads.

Instinctively, I go to do as she says and call her, but then I see that Mum said she is sure it's nothing to worry about. Is it that important, or am I better off going to speak to Kyle and see what might be troubling him?

Deciding that this is a situation in which I should put my husband before my mother, I leave my phone and go to the bathroom to check on my man. When I try the door, I find it unlocked and see my husband standing in front of the mirror. But he's not brushing his teeth or shaving his stubble with a razor. He's simply staring at his reflection in the mirror, which only makes me even more concerned that something is wrong.

'What is it?' I ask him as I approach him at the sink, and he seems surprised when he sees that I have followed him in here.

'Nothing. I'm fine,' he says, grinning, though I know a forced smile when I see one.

'No, there's something bothering you, I can tell,' I say, putting a hand on his shoulder to show that I am here for him. 'What is it? You can tell me.'

'I'm fine, seriously,' Kyle tries again, not convincing anybody. 'I guess I'm just sad that the wedding is over, and we have to go back to work.'

I might have believed that if he had just said it when we woke up because that would have been more natural but not after seeing him staring mournfully at his reflection before pretending like everything was fine in his world.

'Hey, come on. We're married now. No secrets,' I persist, and that seems to be the thing that finally gets Kyle to admit that there is something, before he tells me.

'It's not your problem,' he starts with, but I dismiss that quickly by telling him that as a married couple, we deal with problems together now, not separately.

'It's the business,' he admits a moment later as my hand still rests on his shoulder.

'The business? What about it?'

'There's an issue with one of my clients. He's not paid what he owes us on time, and it's causing a problem because we have a tax bill due, and we can't pay it unless we get the money from him first.'

'How much does he owe you?'

'It's a lot.'

'How much?'

'Over one hundred thousand.'

I can hardly even comprehend the figure Kyle has just said to me, and my hesitation in replying gives my husband the chance to try and downplay its size.

'It's fine, seriously. He'll pay soon enough, and everything will be fine. Don't worry about it,' he says, and the shrug he gives then is almost enough to force my hand from his shoulder. But not quite, and just like I recognised a fake smile when I saw it, I recognise a nervous shrug too.

He's trying to play it cool, but he's anxious, as he should be because that does sound like an awful lot of money.

'Why hasn't he paid you yet?' is my next question.

'Who?'

'This client who owes you all the money! Why hasn't he paid you?'

'Cash flow problems,' Kyle mutters.

'But now he's giving you problems. You need to get him to pay you.'

'I know. I'm trying.'

'Well, try harder!'

I don't mean to shout, but I'm frustrated and a little surprised that I'm having to be so blunt with my husband. He's usually so calm and cool, fully in control and not only that but he's confident enough to always go and get what he wants. Yet, for some reason, here he is, almost cowering in our bathroom and allowing another person to dictate things to him.

'This is your business, and you've worked hard to build it up,' I say, reminding him how proud I am and also how proud of himself he should be. 'You need to fix this problem and then figure out a way to make sure it never happens again. Okay?'

'It's not as simple as that.'

'Why not?'

'I can't just force him to pay. I mean, we have a contract and all that, but if he doesn't have the money then he can't pay, can he? That means I can't pay my tax bill, and HMRC don't care about excuses; they will just punish me.'

'How much is your tax bill?'

'It's six figures as well.'

If I was shocked by the first number I was given, I am just as shocked at this one.

'Your tax bill is that big?'

'Yeah, it's been a good year. Almost too good, if anything.'

Kyle laughs nervously, but I'm not laughing.

'But I don't understand. If you owe so much in tax, you must have made a fortune in profit, so surely you have the money,' I say to him whilst also wondering that if Kyle has hundreds of thousands of pounds somewhere, why hasn't he mentioned this before? I mean, I knew the business was going well, not just because he told me so but because I can see the house we live in and the car he drives, but I had no idea it was that big of a success.

'All my money is tied up in the business,' Kyle explains. 'I can't just access it all and use it whenever I want to. It doesn't work like that. I need it for future growth.'

'Then what are you saying?'

'I'm saying that unless that client pays me what he owes then I can't pay my tax, and if I can't do that, I'll get fined, which I can't afford to pay, and it just goes on and on.'

I'm almost wishing I hadn't asked Kyle what was wrong now because he has certainly enlightened me as to the size of the problem facing him, and now it's my problem too. But I needed to know because we're in everything together these days, good and bad, as we said to each other when we stood at the altar in the presence of loved ones.

'There must be another way,' I say, praying that Kyle actually does know of one. Thankfully, he does.

'The only way is if I got a loan to pay the tax bill and cover me until the client pays up,' he says.

'Okay, do that then,' I cry, relieved there might be a solution after all.

'But I can't do that myself,' Kyle goes on, looking even more sorrowful by the second.

'What?'

'I can't take out a loan in my name.'

'Why not?'

'Because I have something on my record that prevents me from doing it.'

'What do you mean?'

Kyle looks very sheepish now, but I press him for an answer.

'I took out some loans when I was younger,' he admits. 'Back when I was trying to start other businesses. But they didn't work out, and I ended up with a really bad credit rating. No bank will give me a loan anymore. I'm just lucky this business did well, or I'd be destitute.'

That's all news to me, and the first thing I feel is anger that Kyle kept this from me. But seeing how sorry he looks makes it hard to be too mad at him, and what I'd prefer to do is help him find a solution. But before we can talk it through anymore, Kyle tells me that he has to get ready for work and that I'm not to worry about what he has told me because he will figure out a way to make it all okay in the end. Then he walks out of the bathroom and finishes getting dressed before telling me he has to go and we will talk later tonight.

I'm not sure how I'm going to be able to concentrate on my own work today with all that he has said rattling around in my head, but I have to try, so I get myself ready to leave the house before remembering that Mum wanted me to phone her. I'm just about to try her as I make my way to the front door when I see a text message come through from a friend. I haven't spoken to her in a while, not just because she told me that she couldn't make it to my wedding, which was annoying, but also because our busy lives have made it difficult to see each other often before that. But she has reached out to me this morning and when I read her message, I see why.

No sooner have I read what she has sent me then I call Mum, which is what I was about to do anyway, only this time it's not because I need to know what she wants to tell me.

It's because I have something very important to tell her instead.

15

DAWN

'Woah, slow down. What did you say about him?' I ask my daughter as I try to calm the excitable voice at the other end of the line.

'He's out of prison and he's flown to Europe!' Ellie replies, her voice rushed. 'He's in Amsterdam. What's he doing there? Do you think he's going to come here next?'

'Calm down,' I say because it's not easy for me to think when Ellie is so wound up. But she isn't doing as I ask; not the first time my daughter has ignored the advice of her mother.

'It's online! I've just read about it. Harvey is out of prison, and he's already left America,' Ellie cries.

'What do you mean you've just read about it?'

'I'll send you the link now,' Ellie says before the line goes quiet, so I presume she is messaging me. Sure enough, a link arrives on my phone a moment later.

'A friend sent me that,' Ellie explains before I have looked at it properly. 'She said she saw something on social media about it. Apparently, a woman on a flight from LA to Amsterdam was sitting next to Harvey, and she messaged the LA Times as soon as they landed. They have reported on it now.'

I see exactly what Ellie is talking about because when I open the link, I see an article from the LA Times and in it, there is a photo of Harvey in a baseball cap, standing in a line at an airport. Even with the cap on, I recognise him easily, though I'm hardly likely to forget the face of that man, just like I'll never forget the face of his son either.

'What do you think?' Ellie asks me, but I shush her and tell her that I'm reading before concentrating on the article. In it, a reporter has written exactly what my daughter told me. Harvey has been released from prison and, within days, has caught a flight to the Netherlands.

The question is, why has he gone there almost straight from prison?

My first thought is why wouldn't he want to get out and explore the world after so long behind bars? But thinking practically, it does seem strange. Surely he'd be trying to get his life in order after so long off the streets. He'd have mundane, boring life-admin things to do, like sorting out his finances or simply figuring out how to fit back into society. Surely he wouldn't be so relaxed as to just jet off for a city break?

'What's he doing, Mum? Why's he out of prison?' Ellie says, the fear evident in her voice, and it takes me right back to that night in the park not far from here when she almost died at Daryl's hands. I thought she had put that behind her and moved on, but now it sounds like she is right back there again, which only makes me hate that father and son more.

'We always knew he would get released at some point,' I tell my daughter. 'He was guilty of perverting the course of justice but not murder itself, so he wasn't going to spend his whole life in prison. I guess the authorities in America felt he had reformed and served his time and was ready to be allowed out to get on with his life.'

'But I thought he'd stay in LA!' Ellie cries. 'That's so far away from us. But he's in Europe. He could just catch another flight or get on a boat and be here in England soon. Then what if he comes to see us?'

'He wouldn't do that,' I insist, though it's more wishful thinking than fact at this stage.

'He might do! He hates us!' Ellie reminds me, though there was no need for her to do that because I've spent plenty of nights thinking about Harvey and wondering what he would do to me, the woman who killed his son, as well as Ellie, the woman who only just survived his son.

'You need to calm down,' I say, my voice as urgent as my daughter's now. 'Listen to me. Harvey is not going to come here, and he is not going to try and hurt us. He'd be stupid to do that, and besides, I don't think he can come here anyway, not with his criminal record.'

'It doesn't feel right,' Ellie says then, and despite me trying to put her mind at ease, I secretly feel like I agree. But what can I do?

'Just carry on as normal. Don't let him or his son ruin your life,' I say to Ellie, wanting to bring this conversation topic to a close. 'Remember, that was the promise we made to each other five years ago. We weren't going to be defined by that pair. Look how far you've come since. You're married and you have a good job. You are thriving. Don't let Harvey ruin that.'

Ellie goes quiet, which usually means, at that point in an argument, she is giving up and coming around to my way of thinking. But during the brief silence, I am reminded of the fact that there is something troubling me, and it has nothing to do with the past and everything to do with the present. It's Kyle and his house and more specifically, whether or not he is lying to both of us about something.

'What did you want to talk to me about?' Ellie asks then.

'Huh?'

'You sent me a message at one o'clock in the morning saying you needed to talk to me about something. What is it?'

That's right, I did send a message to Ellie, and I did want to talk to her about it as soon as possible. But now, considering the state she has just got herself in over the news about Harvey being in Europe, I'm not sure if I should drop this on her too. At least not over the phone.

'It doesn't matter. It can wait,' I say, figuring another few hours won't be a problem. 'But can you call around my place after work so we can talk then?'

'Why can't you just tell me what it is?'

'It's fine, we can talk later. You need to go to work and so do I.'

'Okay,' Ellie mutters. 'Have a good day.'

'You too, love.' I say just before she hangs up, and I can tell she's annoyed or possibly just still worrying about Harvey being out of prison. I'll admit that has given me something to think about too, on top of Kyle and what he might be up to, and before I know it, I am sitting in front of my laptop again and browsing the internet. Like my daughter, I need to be leaving the house to go to my own workplace, but delaying myself momentarily, I search for something that might help me answer the question that has been conjured up by the news that Harvey is in the Netherlands.

Why there?

It doesn't take me too long to figure it out because I learn that the Netherlands are one of the countries that has no limitations on travellers with criminal records passing through their borders. Is that the only reason Harvey has chosen to go there? Because he wanted a holiday and that was one country to which he was free to travel to without the restrictions that his conviction could impose? Or is there something else to it, like Ellie believes?

Is he just getting as close as he can to England, which is where he really wants to be because we're here?

'No, don't be stupid,' I say out loud to myself. So what if he has made it to Amsterdam without issue? It's not England, and he will still have a hard time getting in here. So he can do whatever he wants to do over there as long as he is in a different country to me and my daughter.

Aware that I really need to leave now or else I will definitely be late for work, I close my laptop, hoping that thoughts of Harvey will disappear from my mind as quickly as the articles I was reading online have vanished too. But that's not quite the case, and even after beginning my latest shift at the supermarket, I find myself thinking about that man and what he might be doing. That's because ever since I killed his son to save Ellie, there has been a nagging voice at the back of my mind that has constantly reminded me of one very potent fact.

If somebody killed my child, could I let them get away with it?

I've always liked to think that I could, given the extenuating circumstances Daryl died in. He was evil, so surely his father can understand why I hurt him. But even if I spawned an evil child, could I forgive if someone hurt them? Or would there be an aching hole left in my life that I would ultimately come to realise might only be filled by revenge?

One thing is for certain - I'm not worrying about Kyle as much now. But I can't still forget about him, which is why I told Ellie to come and see me after work.

We still need to talk about her husband.

I can't be distracted by the last problem.

I need to make sure there isn't a new threat in her life.

16

DAWN

It was less than an hour into my shift when I accidentally dropped the first jar onto the supermarket floor and watched it smash as it hit the ground. It was an hour in when the second jar fell, and it was ninety minutes later when I managed to mistakenly drop a whole box of red wine, causing much destruction on Aisle Seven that took a long time to clean up. So much for stacking the shelves - I was causing chaos for the customers who were milling around with their baskets rather than helping them, which was probably why, after just over two hours of a very inept performance, I was called into my manager's office where I was asked if everything was okay.

I tried to pretend like it was and that the mistakes I'd made during the first portion of my shift weren't going to happen in the next part of it, but my manager could see that I wasn't telling the truth, mainly because I've always been a terrible liar. It might be a good thing that I'm pretty bad at telling a lie because who wants to be known as being good at that? But it didn't help me change my manager's mind when she said I was excused from work for the day because I was clearly not in the right state of mind to be fulfilling my duties at the supermarket.

I panicked at first because I thought I was in danger of losing my job, but I was reassured that me being sent home was simply a kind courtesy being extended to a loyal and usually efficient member of staff. 'Go home, get some rest and come back tomorrow when you're feeling better' was the order I got from my manager, and I took it, though it was only after I'd left work that I realised how distracted I really had been during my shift.

Rather than concentrating on my tasks at hand, I'd been consumed by worries about both Harvey and Kyle and what either man might have been up to. Whenever I tried to forget about one of them, the other one would rear itself in my thoughts, and before I knew it, I'd become stuck in a vicious cycle of thinking all sorts of paranoid things about both of them. Like imagining Kyle was some manipulative liar who had tricked my daughter into marrying him, not for love but for some other unknown reason, and that woman's name on the envelope was actually a secret lover of his. I also imagined Harvey finding his way into England by whatever means he could and coming to visit me or my daughter, telling us that he was doing this for Daryl before attacking one or both of us and making me feel the pain he felt inside over losing his own child.

Needless to say, my manager was right when she detected there was something wrong, and it's a good thing I've left work before any more things got dropped on the floor.

I'll have to apologise to the cleaner tomorrow when I see him because I've certainly kept him busy with my antics today, as well as apologising to my manager too. But that's tomorrow's problem; today I have other things on my plate, and while I can't do much about Harvey and wondering what he is doing, I can tackle the issue of Kyle, and I'm very much looking forward to talking to Ellie when she calls around later.

However, it is as I am driving home that I wonder if it is a good idea to try and uncover more evidence that shows he has been lying. That's how I have the idea to go to the estate agency that apparently owns the property he calls his own to ask them about their tenant. But before I do that, I get spooked at the thought of somebody there potentially calling Kyle after my visit because then he would know that I'm suspicious of him. I need something else.

Then I have it.

Instead of going home and resting like I told my manager I would do, I go to Ellie's place instead. I know she's at work, as is Kyle, and the lack of cars on their driveway confirms that the house is currently empty. But it's not them who I have come here to see.

I want to talk to a neighbour.

Approaching one of the houses next door to where my daughter currently lives with her new husband, I knock on the front door and hope that somebody is home. While I wait to find out, I look around the exterior of the property and think about how this place looks just as nice as all the other houses on this street. It really is a lovely neighbourhood, and it's no surprise that Kyle would want to live here. But why lie and say he owns the house if he rents it? And why lie about that woman too?

The front door suddenly opens, and I'm met with the sight of a small, elderly woman with a friendly face whose eyes examine me from behind a set of round glasses.

'Hello?' she says, a little nervously, as if she's not quite sure if she's just inadvertently answered her door to a saleswoman who she won't be able to get rid of easily. But I quickly reassure her that I'm not here to try and get her to part with some of her money – rather, I'm simply here as a relative of one of her neighbours.

'Hi, I'm Ellie's mother,' I say with a big smile on my face. 'You know, Ellie next door.'

'Ahh yes,' the woman says with an equally big smile. 'Nice to meet you. Is everything okay?'

'Yes, it is, thank you for asking. It's just I have been next door helping tidy a few things up, and I found some post for a woman under the name of Julia Beaumont. I was wondering if it might have been meant for one of Ellie's neighbours. Do you know of anyone by that name?'

'No, sorry,' the woman replies. 'There's nobody on this street under that name.'

'I see. Perhaps it was the woman who used to live in the house before Kyle moved in,' I go on, but again, the woman has a clear answer for me there.

'No, the previous occupant was not called Julia,' the woman tells me.

'Are you sure?'

'Yes, I am. I've lived here for over fifty years, ever since these houses were first built, and I can name almost every person who has lived on this street. There's never been a Julia.'

'Oh, I see,' pretending to look puzzled while also resolute now in the knowledge that Kyle lied to me.

'It must have just been sent to the wrong address,' the woman says, and I agree with her.

'One more thing,' I say before I can allow this kind neighbour to get on with her day. 'Have you enjoyed having Kyle as a neighbour? I suspect you have. He's a lovely man, isn't he?'

'He is very nice,' the neighbour confirms. 'Very handsome too.'

I chuckle as she winks at me.

'Much nicer than the last lot,' the neighbour says to me.

'Who was that?'

'Some family who made lots of noise and didn't maintain their garden. Very frustrating. I was glad when Kyle moved in a few months ago.'

'Only a few months ago?' I repeat, confused.

'Yes, that's right. He moved in, and then Ellie joined him not long after that. But you already know this, don't you.'

'Oh, yes, of course,' I say before thanking the woman and being on my way. But as I walk away from her house, I think about how I have just caught Kyle in another lie. He has told both me and Ellie that he has lived in this house for a couple of years.

Why more lies? What is he hiding?

I don't have time to think about that because no sooner have I got back to the road then I see Kyle's car coming right towards me.

There's no way for either of us to not see the other one, and he very slowly parks on his driveway before getting out and looking confused at my presence here.

'Dawn? Is everything okay?' he asks me.

'Err, yes. Is everything okay with you? I thought you'd be at work.'

'Oh right, yeah, erm, I was feeling a little bit under the weather, so I came home early. What are you doing here?'

'Erm, I was just passing and thought I'd see if anyone was home. But of course, Ellie is at work, isn't she?'

'That's right. Anything I can help with?'

I'm tempted to just say no and get back in my car and leave, but now Kyle is standing right in front of me, I see this as an opportunity for him to put to bed any of the doubts I am having about him. There has to be a logical explanation for his lies, so let's see what it is.

'There is one thing, actually,' I say, and Kyle doesn't look thrilled about that, probably because he's eager to get inside and was not expecting his mother-in-law to be lurking on his street when he got home.

'What's that?'

'It's a bit of a personal question, actually. I hope you don't mind, but I was wondering, how much did you pay for this house?'

Kyle frowns for a moment.

'Why? Do you want to buy it from me?' he asks with a cheeky grin.

'Haha. No, I was just wondering. I'm trying to get an idea of house prices in certain areas.'

'You're moving?'

'Possibly. One day. Maybe. So how much is it to buy around here?'

'Oh, erm. I can't remember the exact figure now, but I can check and get back to you,' Kyle says, which doesn't sound convincing at all.

Who doesn't remember how much they paid for their house?

'Okay, no problem,' I say, feeling even worse now. 'I guess prices have changed a lot in the two years since you bought it. It was two years, right?'

'That's right,' Kyle says, doubling down on his lie. 'Sorry, I'm not feeling too well, like I said, so I think I'm going to go and have a lie down. Is that okay?'

'Yes, of course. You go and get some rest. I'll see you soon,' I say with a smile before walking back to my car, and as I get in it, I see Kyle entering the house. But it's not *his house*. I know that now.

He's a tenant.

He's also a liar.

Checking the time, I figure that it's only a few more hours until Ellie finishes work, and then she is coming to see me, allowing me to tell her what I know, and then it's up to her to decide what to do about it.

As I drive away, I make one more glance at the house as I pass it and when I do, I see Kyle inside the property. He is standing at the window watching me go. But he doesn't wave at me, and I don't wave either.

Perhaps he senses that something is wrong. If so, he would be right.

I am sensing something too.

I'm getting déjà vu about Ellie and her choice of partners.

17

HARVEY

Amsterdam is a nice place, but it's not where I want to be. Instead of being beside all these canals and watching locals and tourists pedalling around on bicycles, I want to be on my way to England, where Dawn and Ellie reside. But rather than wasting time in this pretty city, I am doing something about that.

As everyone knows, there are two sides to a place like Amsterdam. It all depends on what a person is looking for, but like Las Vegas, a person can usually find whatever it is they desire if they look in the right places. I've been on the hunt for what I want ever since I got off the plane here, and that search led me to some interesting places. Considering what I want is not legal, I figured the best way of finding it was to visit places that criminals might frequent. I'm talking backstreet bars and brothels, seedy underground clubs and the types of venues where the clientele are just as grim as the weather can be in this part of Europe in winter. It was last night, while I was having a drink in a bar full of scantily clad women and heavily tattooed men, when I asked the barman a question I had been asking all over town ever since I got here.

'I need passage into England. Do you know anybody who could help?'

The question was a simple one, and I figured that as long as I didn't ask it to an undercover police officer, then I would eventually get what I was looking for. Of course, I wouldn't know the person was an undercover officer until it was too late, but I could reduce the chances of falling afoul of the law by observing the people I asked until I was confident they really were who they were pretending to be.

After asking the barman the question, I had been expecting one of two answers. Either he would tell me he couldn't help me or he would tell me to get lost. That's what everyone else I had asked so far had said to me. But this time, I got a more interesting answer.

After being told that he might be able to help, I was advised to go down a corridor at the back of the bar and see the man in the office there. Nervous at what might be waiting for me but aware these were exactly the kind of tricky situations I'd have to go through to find myself a person capable of smuggling me into the UK, I walked down the corridor and knocked on the door. No sooner had I opened it then I was pulled inside and searched, a burly man with a shaved head examining me for any recording devices or identification. When they were satisfied that I wasn't an undercover officer myself, they asked me to confirm what it was I wanted. After I did that, they gave me a price.

Hearing that the price was one I could afford was almost as much of a relief as the fact that I left that office without being harmed, and as I made my way out of the bar, nodding at the barman as I went, I had done what I'd set out to do.

I'd arranged to be transported to England discreetly, very illegally, but hopefully, successfully.

That was last night, and I've spent today on a coach making my way south out of Amsterdam and down to a port just north of Rotterdam, which is where I have been told to meet the people who will smuggle me on board a van that will be transported across the North Sea on a ferry. It's incredibly risky, but if it works, I will arrive on the southeast coast of England, and it won't be far at all then to get to Suffolk and see the two people I want to pay a visit to.

As I sat on the coach, I had plenty of time to think about things, in particular, the fact that the woman I saw on the plane from America contacted the LA Times and told them I was out of prison and in Europe now. Having a nosey busybody like that interfering in my affairs is not particularly welcome and neither is my name being mentioned online again in various media outlets, but it couldn't be helped. I did wonder if Dawn and Ellie had seen the reports though, and if so, they must be wondering what I'm doing over on this side of the Atlantic.

They'll find out soon enough.

After disembarking the coach and walking the rest of the way, I have found myself in a disused car park about ten minutes away from the port. In the distance, I can see huge vessels coming in to dock and enormous shipping containers being loaded onto a few of them. It looks to be a very busy place and is sure to have plenty of security staff on duty there, so I hope the people I have come to meet know what they are doing.

Fifteen minutes of standing in this car park by myself has me wondering if I am in the right place, or worse, if I've just been told false information and have wasted my time. But then I see a large white van enter the car park, and it comes to a stop in front of me. The driver quickly gets out and asks me for my name, which I give, before he asks if I have the money.

'Yes,' I say, reaching into my jacket pocket before producing the envelope full of cash that matches the amount I was quoted back in Amsterdam.

The driver checks it quickly before stuffing it into his own jacket and then opening up the back of the van.

'Get in,' he orders me, clearly a man of few words, but neither of us are here to make friends, so I do as he says and walk to the back of the van. When I look inside, I see several fridge freezers, some standing up against the sides of the van, others lying on their sides.

'Hurry up,' the man tells me, and it's clear that I'm supposed to climb in and hide amongst these utility items.

I pull myself into the back of the van and sit down on one of the fridges, but the driver tells me that is no good and orders me to go to the back and get behind the fridges there. I do as he says, assuming he has done this sort of thing many times before and must have been successful if he is still doing it. Then I get a shock when I realise I'm not the only person he is going to be transporting today.

I see the nervous face peering up at me from behind the fridge I have just climbed over and it's the face of a young man in his early twenties, and he looks very timid as he sees me joining him. I'm about to ask him who he is when I see the driver going to shut the door, so just before he does, I have a question for him.

'How does this work? How long will we have to be in here for?' I ask, but the driver completely ignores me and slams the back doors shut, plunging us into total darkness.

'Just stay quiet,' a voice says beside me, one with an Eastern European accent, and I guess my fellow passenger here today is no stranger to travelling by these kinds of means.

It's so dark that I cannot even see my hand in front of my face, never mind the face of the man sitting beside me, so there's not much I can do other than take his advice and stay quiet. But any talking we might have been doing would have been drowned out anyway a moment later when the engine restarts and the van is put into motion.

It's loud in here, still dark and now, very bumpy.

I reach out and put my hand on the side of the fridge before trying to stretch out my legs as best I can to get comfortable for the long journey ahead. I have no idea how long I'll have to hide back here because the driver wasn't kind enough to tell me, but I figure it's going to be a while before these doors open again and I can step outside. When they do open, I can only hope it's the driver I see ushering me out and not a bunch of stern-looking customs officials, but that remains to be seen.

This is it.

We're on our way to the port.

Next stop - England.

Hopefully.

18

DAWN

Having been left unsettled by my most recent interaction with Kyle, one in which he did absolutely nothing to dispel any of my doubts about him, I have spent the afternoon waiting impatiently for Ellie to finish work and come and see me, as she promised, so that we can talk. In that time, I have been rehearsing what I want to say because I don't want to make the mistake of going about this the wrong way and having Ellie feel like I am overreacting or judging her husband. I just want to simply state the things I have recently discovered and let her know that there might be a perfectly reasonable explanation behind it all, but it's one that she needs to seek out, and I will be happy to help her with that. In fact, I'd prefer it if she did want me to help her question Kyle about some of his lies because that would mean she wouldn't be alone with him when she did it.

Who knows how he will react to being called a liar? He might panic and lash out. However, one thing I am telling myself over and over again is that he is not Daryl. Very few people in the world are wired like that dangerous American was, so whatever happens next, I'm sure it won't be as bad as it was before.

Right?

The time is five o'clock now, and I know Ellie will be finishing work and leaving the office promptly. Bless her, she's never exactly been one to do overtime and go the extra mile, as it were, preferring to just fulfil her obligations and get home to where life is more fun. I can't blame her there, and I am hoping that today is no different because I want her here now, as quickly as possible.

Then I get a message from her.

'Sorry, Mum. I forgot I said I'd go for leaving drinks tonight with a friend from work. Can't get out of it! Can I come around tomorrow instead?'

Ellie's text is not what I wanted to read because while it sounds like she innocently double-booked herself tonight, what I have to say to her is far more important than any leaving drinks with colleagues. That's why I try calling her, but annoyingly, she doesn't answer.

'Ellie. Sorry, but I really need to talk to you. Can you get out of it? Or come to mine after?'

I press send but then receive no reply, and I wonder if Ellie's phone is now back in her handbag and she's already in a bar somewhere near her office having her first drink with her work friends. Maybe I could try and find her and talk to her there. Is that a bit too dramatic of me to turn up and say what I have to say in front of the people she works with? It would certainly spoil her evening and because of that, I doubt Ellie would be very happy with me, even if what I had to tell her was important. But what else can I do? Sit here and do nothing?

I decide to get my coat and go for a walk, telling myself that I will just get some fresh air but also aware that I may quickly find myself heading into town and in the direction of a few of the pubs that are near where I know Ellie works. If I happen to bump into my daughter somewhere along the way, then so be it.

But just before I can leave my house, I open my door and see a car parking at the top of my driveway. It's Maggie, and while this is an unexpected visit from my friend, it is nice to see her. I just wish her timing had been better.

'Hi! You're not going out, are you?' Maggie asks as she sees me standing in the doorway with my coat on.

'Erm, I was actually.'

'Where are you going? Anywhere exciting?'

'Erm,' I say, stalling because I don't want to say that I'm about to go looking for my daughter and ruin her night because I'm worried about her husband's lies.

'Wait a minute? Are you going on a date?' Maggie asks me, her face lighting up with excitement. But I shoot down that idea quickly.

'A date? No way,' I say, thinking about how she still doesn't know about my disastrous evening with John because I haven't told anybody about that yet.

'Well, maybe I can change that for you,' Maggie says unexpectedly. 'There is a guy in my office who I think might be perfect for you. He's called Chris; he's divorced, though not through any fault of his own. He's looking to start dating again, and, best of all, he's devilishly handsome! What do you say?'

I feel like saying I'm not sure because my first instinct is to avoid any more dates for a while. But then I figure that it can't do any harm to say yes, especially when my friend clearly thinks this guy is perfect for me.

'Does he know my history?' I ask Maggie, and she surprises me by saying that he does, admitting to it being gossiped about in her office at the time it happened, though only in a good way, of course.

I roll my eyes at that, but the fact Chris knows who I am and what I did before and still wants to go out with me sounds promising, so with that, Maggie agrees to set up the date.

'I'll leave you to it then. I know you're busy,' Maggie says, turning back to her car, but just before she goes, I have something to tell her.

'Ellie's husband is lying,' I say despondently.

'What?' Maggie looks confused. 'What about?'

'All sorts of things.'

'Is he cheating on her?'

'No. At least I don't think so.'

'What did Ellie say?'

'She doesn't know yet. I'm trying to tell her in person.'

'Tell her what?'

'That Kyle is a liar!'

I expect Maggie to be on my side, but she is frowning now.

'What?' I ask her nervously.

'Kyle? As in the wonderful man I just witnessed her marrying in Turkey?' Maggie states. 'Are you sure?'

'Yes, I know he seems perfect, and I thought he was too, but I have caught him lying about things, and Ellie needs to know.'

'What things? Big things?'

'He doesn't own his house. He rents it.'

'Okay,' Maggie muses. 'That's an issue, but it's not the end of the world. What else?'

'He lied about a woman's name on an envelope.'

'A woman's name on an envelope?'

Maggie is now looking at me like I'm overreacting, which is strange because I thought she'd be on my side. Then she explains herself.

'Look, I get you're scarred from what happened with Daryl, but you can't not trust any of Ellie's partners,' she says. 'They're not all going to be serial killers.'

'Yes, I know that, thank you,' I say sarcastically. 'I'm not saying he's a serial killer. I'm just saying that he has been lying about a few things.'

'Minor things.'

'He shouldn't be lying at all!'

'I guess not,' Maggie agrees. 'But be careful.'

'What do you mean?'

'I mean Ellie is very fragile,' Maggie reminds me. 'You know it's been hard for you to trust any of her partners since Daryl, but imagine what it's been like for her. It must be a million times harder. So imagine the strength it has taken for her to fall in love with Kyle and get married to him with all those past anxieties rattling around in her head. She's incredibly brave and strong, and from what I have seen of her recently, she is thriving.'

'So what's your point?'

'My point is that you have to be very careful before you go and give her a new reason to stop trusting again,' Maggie says, her empathy clearly coming through. 'Make absolutely certain that Kyle is really up to something bad or don't interfere because if you do and it turns out to be nothing, you risk losing Ellie and even worse than that, you risk setting her back to the point where she stops being the happy adult she has become and you take her back to being your little girl, scared and alone.'

'I'm just trying to be a good mother,' I say, figuring that much was obvious, and Maggie nods to show that she understands, but she reminds me to be careful.

'If you think something is wrong, trust your intuition,' my friend tells me. 'It was right last time, so maybe it's right again. But if Kyle is lying then there is a reason, and if you really want to find out what it is, having Ellie confront him might not be the best way.'

'What are you saying?'

'He could just deny it. Shell up. Then you'll never know. I'm saying if you want the truth about him, focus on him, not your daughter. Then you'll really know if there is anything to worry about or not.'

19

DAWN

Maggie's words of advice were ringing in my ears all of last night, especially when Ellie phoned me back after her drinks with work friends had finished. She wanted to know what it was that was so important for me to tell her, and that was my moment to relay the information that I knew Kyle was lying about the house and some woman called Julia Beaumont. But I didn't do it because, as Maggie had advised, throwing a hand grenade like that into my daughter's relationship when I wasn't fully sure of all the facts myself might not have been the best way to deal with the situation.

That's why I told her that it didn't matter before I changed the subject and asked her how her night had been. She told me that she had had a wonderful time and admitted to being a little tipsy before saying she was excited to be on her way home to Kyle. I nervously nibbled my lip then, pleased that my daughter was so happy but also aware that I could ruin that if I spoke up. But I stayed quiet, allowing Ellie to carry on in her blissful state, although I'm not being neglectful and allowing Kyle's lies to pass by without further investigation.

Maggie suggested I focus on him, for the time being, rather than my daughter, and that's what I intend to do.

That's why I'm going to follow him this morning.

I'm currently sitting in my car at the end of Ellie and Kyle's street, and I'm waiting for them to emerge from their home to begin their day. I have already phoned in sick from work today, using yesterday's 'incident' to add strength to my claim that I'm not feeling well and need another twenty-four hours to get back to my normal self. But instead of resting at my house with a hot water bottle and some medication, I am ready to follow Kyle and see if I can catch him in any more lies, eager to know if his lies stop here or if he has been spinning a whole web of deceit ever since he met my daughter.

It's just past eight o'clock, and this is around the time I know Ellie usually leaves for work. Kyle often goes before her, and I have been waiting for him so I can tail him, but, so far, neither of them have emerged from the house. Is everything alright? *Yes, stop panicking*, I tell myself. Then I wonder if Ellie might be hungover after last night's drinks and if so, she might not be going to work today. Is Kyle going to stay home with her? If he does, I'm not going to have much luck following him. But then I see their front door open, and Kyle strides out, looking smart in a white shirt, navy blue trousers and a dark tie. He's clearly ready for work and so is Ellie because she is right behind him.

I watch as the pair get into his car, which is the only one they could get in because Ellie's vehicle isn't here. I'm guessing it's still at her office where she must have left it before going out for drinks and taking a cab home. That's my girl. *Sensible.*

Once they're in the car, Kyle reverses off the drive, and they head off along the street in the opposite direction to me. But I'm quickly following them, maintaining a safe distance so they won't see me but making sure not to lose them either as we reach the main road and join the bulk of the commuter-filled traffic.

I quickly realise we are heading in the direction of Ellie's office, and it's good of Kyle to drop his wife off at work before going to his workplace. I wonder what they are talking about on route. Perhaps they are discussing what to have for dinner tonight, or maybe they are debating which TV series to start next. I hope it's simple, fun stuff like that rather than anything too heavy. But there might be a time for a very serious conversation soon, depending on what I discover about Kyle today, and as I watch him wave Ellie off after she has got out of his car, I guess I'm about to find out.

As Ellie goes into her office and I set off again following her husband, I feel shameful that I'm doing something like this. But I'm also following my intuition, and like Maggie the wise sage said: it wasn't wrong last time, and it might not be wrong again.

As I follow Kyle's car, I'm wondering what I will do if I see him simply go to work. Sit in my car all day and wait to see if he does anything else? Or give up and accept that just because he's told a few lies before, he isn't some devious character living a life of deception? I guess I'll find out when I see where Kyle is actually going.

The traffic is growing heavier now as more and more vehicles clog up the roads, everybody in a rush to get to where they need to be before the clock strikes nine. But funnily enough, Kyle doesn't seem to be in much of a rush himself. He's closely adhering to the speed limit, isn't rushing through the amber lights before they turn red, nor does he seem particularly bothered to be sitting in traffic jams because I can see him tapping away on his steering wheel, and at one point, I think he even sings along to the song on the radio.

He looks content enough, but it's a bit of a contrast from the image he portrays at home because whenever I've been there, he always seems to be on his phone, sorting out some deal and telling Ellie how much work he has got on. If he's that busy, surely he'd be keener to get to where he is going.

Eventually, after another ten minutes of crawling along in a queue, I see Kyle indicate to turn left and after following him, I see him parking outside what looks like a Chinese takeaway, although it's not open at this time of day and that's clear because the shutters are down. But as Kyle gets out of his car, it's obvious he's not going to the takeaway; he's going to the door beside it, and after he knocks on the door, he waits for it to be opened.

What is this place? I'm wondering as I stare through my windscreen about twenty yards or so away from where my daughter's husband stands. Then I see the door open, and a woman appears. She smiles when she sees Kyle and he smiles too, but that's not all that happens.

I watch as the woman grabs his tie and pulls him inside, and just before the door closes, I see the pair of them kiss.

Feeling an incredible amount of rage boiling up inside of me, I have the rather idiotic idea to hit the accelerator pedal and ram my car right into that door, which would certainly cause the two occupants on the other side of it to have quite a shock. But I don't do that because it would be stupid and extremely dangerous. All I do is squeeze the steering wheel with both hands and try to process the fact that my daughter is married to a cheat.

Kyle has another woman.

It's lie after lie after lie.

He's clearly not the man either I or Ellie thought he was.

There is no doubting it now.

My intuition was right.

This relationship needs to end.

Desperately upset for my recently married daughter, I think about the effect a divorce will have on her as well as the impossibility of her trusting another man again. Daryl tried to kill her and now Kyle has been having an affair. She's cursed in love, seemingly destined not to have relationships work out for her, and while I don't know why that it is, I do know that she does not deserve any of it.

As the anger I feel towards Kyle continues to bubble away inside of me unchecked, I think about phoning Ellie right now and telling her what I saw. Then I wonder if I should perhaps wait for Kyle to re-emerge, when I could potentially take a photo or capture a video of him in a tryst with this random woman. That would be concrete evidence that I could show to Ellie, and perhaps that is what I need because I would hate for Kyle to talk himself out of this. He is good with words - those words anchored by his good looks - but I won't allow him to weasel his way out of this one, which is why I get my phone ready and prepare to record him leaving this place.

I end up waiting with my camera poised for over an hour, but I don't take my eyes off the door in any of that time because I don't want to miss his reappearance. When the door does open again, I see the man I welcomed into my family step outside, and he is re-adjusting his tie as he goes, suggesting his clothes were removed while he was inside. That makes me feel sick, but I keep my composure long enough to press record and film whatever happens next. I'm glad I do because before Kyle can walk back to his car, the mystery woman reaches out and pulls him back, and the two of them share a long, lingering kiss.

Got you, you cheating bastard.

As Kyle breaks off from his mistress and returns to his vehicle, I make sure the video has been saved on my phone before I think about what to do with it next. Obviously, Ellie needs to see it as soon as possible, but it would be too cruel to just send it to her in a message. I need to show her this in person so that I can be there to comfort her in the immediate aftermath. I guess I'm going to her office then, where I will ask to speak to her and then, sadly, have a very grim discussion with her outside her workplace, one in which her seemingly perfect marriage will come crashing down around her in an instant.

As I watch Kyle driving away, I wonder where he is going next. I wonder if he even has a busy job like he pretends to have. Does he even work, or does he just come here while Ellie thinks he is earning money for them both? How does he pay for what he has? What kind of weird double life is he living?

I don't know, but before I drive away, I'm so consumed with anger that I decide to make the first chink in the armour of this man's carefully constructed charade. I bet the woman he has just visited has no idea what kind of a man he is either. I bet she doesn't know he is married and dropped another woman off at work before coming to visit her. Unless she does know and she doesn't care that Kyle is cheating on my daughter, in which case, I think I need to say a few choice words to her.

Marching towards the front door, I am going to find out if the woman inside deserves my sympathy or my anger, and after knocking, I wait impatiently for an answer. As the door opens, I see the woman who was just planting her lips on my son-in-law, and she frowns as she regards me on her doorstep.

'Hello? Can I help you?' she asks me.

'Maybe you can,' I say, but just before I go on, I'm interrupted by a postman delivering a letter to this same address.

'Good morning,' the polite postie says as he rummages in the bag that hangs over his shoulder before he produces a letter and hands it to the woman who just opened the door. But as he passes it to her, I catch sight of the name on the front.

Julia Beaumont.

So this is her.

'I'm sorry, can I help you?' Julia asks me again, and I just blurt out the first thing that comes to my mind.

'Tell that lying man of yours to stay away from my daughter!'

Then I'm gone, striding back to my car and preparing to speed away in the direction of Ellie's office.

20

ELLIE

One of the perks of having a job that doesn't require me to work too hard is that I can waste a lot of time on the internet when my manager isn't looking at me. That's what I've spent much of the first hour of the day doing today, even though I know I shouldn't because I'm not looking at anything that is making me feel good.

While some of my equally-as-lazy colleagues around me look at fun things like last night's football results or celebrity gossip straight from Hollywood, I am busy reading about Harvey and the articles that talk about him being in the Netherlands. I'm still greatly troubled by the fact he was seen flying to Europe after his release from prison, and despite Mum telling me not to worry about it, that is easier said than done.

He is up to something; I just know it.

The question is, *what?*

The wedding ring on my finger should be a reminder, if I need it, that my life has moved on since I was with Daryl, and I tell myself to focus on Kyle instead of my dead ex-boyfriend's dad. But I know I won't be able to relax until I find a news article that says Harvey is back in Los Angeles because then, I'll know there is a big distance between us once again, and that will mean it is less likely he is coming after me or Mum. Alas, there are no such articles saying anything of the sort, which means I can only think that Harvey is still in

Amsterdam or somewhere around there. But he could be on the move, and it just might not be reported this time.

Is he coming to England? Is he already here?

What is he doing?

Before I can waste away more of my morning pondering that question, the phone on my desk rings, and that snaps me back into work mode.

'Hello?' I say, preparing to have to do something boring and menial now when I find out which one of my colleagues is calling me to ask for something.

'Hey, Ellie. It's Meg on reception. There's somebody here to see you. Can you come down?' comes the cheery voice at the other end of the line.

'Oh, okay,' I say, quickly shutting down the internet pages on my computer screen so my boss won't see them when he passes my desk while I'm away from it. 'On my way!'

I'm quite glad to get the chance to stretch my legs and have a little time away from my desk. Usually, I have to go and stand in the kitchen and make a coffee or visit the bathroom to have a five-minute break, but as I go downstairs, I realise I didn't ask Megan who it was who wanted to see me.

I doubt it's anybody exciting, probably just a courier dropping off a parcel. More admin for me to process. *Yay.*

But then I walk into the reception area and see who it is, and I was not expecting this.

'Kyle! What are you doing here?' I ask my husband. 'Is everything okay?'

'Errr, not really. Can I talk to you outside?' Kyle asks, and I can see that he looks very nervous about something, so I quickly agree.

Smiling at Megan to make out like everything is fine, I follow my husband outside.

'What's happened? Why aren't you at work?' I ask him, and Kyle shakes his head.

'I've got a problem,' he admits. 'It's that one I told you about, remember?'

'The client who hasn't paid what he owes?'

'Yeah. It's all messed up. I can't afford to keep the business going!'

'What?'

'I need £100,000 in the next twenty-four hours or it's over,' Kyle cries. 'I lose everything. All my hard work gone to waste. I don't know what to do.'

It's awful to see my usually confident man burying his head in his hands and clearly looking so distressed, and in this moment, I would do anything to help him.

'I can give you the money my dad left for me,' I suggest. 'It's not much, but he left it for a time when I needed it, and this is for both of us, so I can use it.'

'Thank you, it would be a start. But it's nowhere near enough. I need more.'

It could be a little dismissive of Kyle to disregard the £5,000 that my father saved and left for me after his death, but I know it's only because he's so desperate.

'Then what about a loan?' I suggest.

'I told you, I can't take it out in my name because of my credit history.'

'Then why don't I take it out in my name?'

Kyle stops pacing around and stares at me after my suggestion, and I nod my head to show him that I was serious about it.

'I'll take out the loan myself, and you can use the money to save the business. You can pay it back when the client pays, and everything will be okay, right?'

'No, Ellie, it's too much. I can't ask you to do that for me.'

'You haven't asked me. I have decided it,' I say, feeling nervous because of how much money we are talking about here but also pleased because I can see my suggestion could solve my husband's problem.

'I have a good credit rating. I'm employed. I have savings. They'll give me a loan,' I say. 'I could go to the bank right now and do it if I can get out of work for a short while.'

Kyle stares at me like I am the best wife in the world, which is exactly what I aim to be, so I just smile back at him and repeat again that it is no problem.

'Wow, you're amazing,' Kyle says, genuinely thrilled that I have offered to help him. 'But only if you're sure? And you know we can pay it all back and the interest, don't worry about that. You won't end up out of pocket, I swear.'

'Hey, we're a team,' I remind him. 'It's not about who owes who; it's about both of us working together to make things work. Okay?'

Kyle nods his head, and then I give him a hug because he sure looks like he needs one. I've never seen him as stressed as this, but he is already looking much better, although we're not quite there yet.

'I could go to the bank on my lunch break?' I suggest, and after checking his phone, Kyle says that will be fine.

'Thank you so much,' he says before giving me another hug, but I tell him to stop worrying now and focus on getting that client to pay what they owe while I sort out the money to tide the business over in the meantime.

'I got so lucky when I married you,' Kyle says with a big grin on his face, and I laugh before completely agreeing with him. Then he heads back to his car, and I return to the office, smiling again at Megan as I pass her before making it back upstairs and to my desk.

Checking the clock in the corner of my computer screen, I see that there are still two hours to go until I can officially call it lunchtime, so I will have to impatiently wait until then. To kill a little bit of time, I check my phone but have no new messages there. I consider texting Mum and telling her what I am about to do in terms of the bank loan, but I wonder if she will think it is a bad idea and try to talk me out of it. She might say that it is too much money, but while that is true, I know what I am doing. Kyle will be able to pay it back, and, in the meantime, we can keep on top of the interest payments. If worst comes to worst, I have Dad's money that can go towards some of it, but it won't come to that because

Kyle's client will pay, and then the loan will be gone, and the business will be saved.

The way I see it, I'm doing what any wife would do. I am helping my husband, and I know he'd do the same for me if the roles were reversed.

Putting my phone away, I know this is all going to be fine, and I can't wait to have that money so that Kyle stops worrying. Getting back to work with renewed focus, I am glad I have been distracted from thinking about Harvey. I'm also glad I didn't message Mum.

She doesn't need to know everything, I think.

I'm capable of making adult decisions myself.

She's got enough of her own problems.

Unfortunately, at that time, I had no idea just how much that last one was true.

21

DAWN

Silly me. Foolish me. Stupid me.

I thought I was the clever one. I thought I was too experienced, too worn down by life to be tricked into something. Ellie still maintains much of her innocence of youth, which I wonder if that is the reason why she continually falls for the lies of other people and ends up getting hurt. But not me. I thought I was capable of seeing through people with bad intentions.

I guess I used to be.

But not anymore.

I know I've been tricked because I'm sitting on the carpet in the living area of a very modest flat, and my wrists are tied together to the base of the radiator behind me, wrapped tightly in one of the ties Kyle presumably wears when he is pretending to be going to work. I've just been assaulted, and now I'm being held prisoner, and there are only two things I can do at the moment.

One is to continue to keep silently cursing myself for my stupidity.

The second is to stare at the woman who is holding me and wish a million hateful things upon her.

Sensing that my eyes are boring into her, my captor leaves the room briefly, presumably because it's easier for her to keep me here if she doesn't have to be around me all the time. But not wanting to make this any easier for her, I call out after her, reminding her that she is in big trouble and that she won't get away with this, meaning there will be no respite to be found in whatever room she has disappeared into now. She soon comes back, which is what I wanted, though what she has in her hands is not what I want to see. She is still holding a knife, which is a weapon she's been brandishing ever since I first realised I was in trouble here. But she is now also holding a tea towel, and it's clear she wants to use that second item to shut me up.

'I'll remind you again,' Julia says as she stands over me. 'You try to hurt me or make another sound or do anything to ruin this for me and Kyle, then you will never see your daughter again. Got it?'

Such a threat is surely enough to make any mother comply, but before I can be silenced, I have a question, and it's one I've already asked several times since I found myself in this situation.

'Please, just tell me what you want, and I can get it for you. Leave Ellie alone. She doesn't deserve this. What is it? What are you trying to do here?'

However, just like the other times I asked for a motive, Julia ignores me and makes sure to show me the knife one more time before wrapping the tea towel around my head, making sure the front portion of it is in and across my mouth, which will stifle any noises I try to make in future.

I wriggle to show my contempt for my treatment but don't fight back as fully as I might be able to, mainly because I know I can't escape anyway but also because I can't risk Julia using the knife on me or hurting Ellie because of my revolt.

As Julia finishes what she is doing, she steps back and admires her work, and she seems satisfied that she has gone a little further in keeping her prisoner under control.

That's what I am now.

A prisoner.

How did I let this happen?

Sadly, I know the answer to that one, which is why I know it is all my fault, and I played right into my captor's hands. Doing one little thing differently could have made a huge difference and made it almost impossible for me to end up in this situation, but I played this all wrong, and now I am paying the price.

I never should have got out of my car after seeing Kyle leaving this flat. I had the evidence of him kissing this woman saved on my phone, and that was all I needed to show to Ellie to ruin him and end the sham of their marriage. I could have just driven away, and this would have been over. But I didn't, unwisely opting to leave my car after Kyle had driven away because I was so consumed with anger and going to tell the woman in the flat that the man she was involved with was already involved with another woman. I was doing it to get back at Kyle, to ultimately ruin both his relationship with Ellie and his mistress, leaving him with no one.

But I made a mistake.

After discovering the mistress in question was Julia, the woman who Kyle had received some mail for at his current home, I told her that her lying man was to stay away from my daughter. Then I turned my back to her and walked to my car, anger emanating through every pore of my body as I prepared to go and break my daughter's heart with the bad news about what her husband was really up to behind her back. But I hadn't got far because Julia called after me, begging me to explain what I was talking about, and she grabbed my arm and pulled me back to her.

As I had turned around, I hadn't seen a clever, calculating woman staring back at me. I had seen a confused, anxious and fearful woman who seemed to have absolutely no idea what was going on, and she looked exactly how I imagined Ellie would look when I told her that Kyle was having an affair soon. Julia begged me to tell her what I was talking about, saying she didn't understand why I was at her flat or why I was so angry at Kyle.

So I told her. I said that Kyle was married to my daughter and was clearly lying to her, which was news to Julia, or so I thought at the time, because she put her hands to her mouth and looked devasted. She even called Kyle a "lying rat", which only made me think we were both on the same side even more, allowing me to lower my guard further.

Stupid, stupid woman I think to myself as I reflect on the charade I fell for, not that it does me any good in hindsight.

As I'd stood in front of a mortified Julia, she insisted that she wasn't the bad guy here and had no idea Kyle was married to another woman. I thought she was being honest, though it didn't do much to make up for the hurt coming my daughter's way shortly. But then Julia's shock seemed to subside, and it was replaced by anger, and she told me that if Kyle had been lying to her too, she wanted to help me ruin him. I could see she meant it, though I had no idea what she had in mind. That was until she told me she had to show me something, and she went back into her flat then, telling me that what she had in mind would prove to me what a bad guy Kyle had been.

I had watched her disappear through her front door and waited a moment for her to return, my mind racing with possibilities about what I was going to be shown. I know I could have just left then and given up the chance to see what Julia wanted to show me, but as I stood there by her door, I was aware that very soon, my daughter was going to be embroiled in divorce proceedings. Things like that can be messy and not always fair, and Kyle could make things ugly. Therefore, if there was something I could be shown that would further enhance Ellie's position and make her even more of a victim whilst simultaneously weakening Kyle's position during the divorce proceedings then I felt I had to see it.

I'd called out to Julia when she had failed to re-emerge after a minute, but she hadn't replied, making me wonder what was going on. That was the moment I stepped towards the doorway to call out and tell her not to worry about it because I'd rather just be getting on my way and if need be, I could always return at some point once my daughter had been informed about this crazy situation. But as I looked into the doorway, I saw Julia on her knees and sobbing greatly, her whole body shaking, and my heart broke for her because she was clearly a woman whose life had just been turned upside down by me coming to her door this morning.

The motherly instinct in me quickly took over, and I went inside to try and comfort her, telling her as I went that Kyle was the one to blame and she would feel better once we had exposed him for the liar he is. But no sooner had I got close to her then Julia revealed her own lies, and by the time I saw that she had been faking her tears, it was already too late.

She'd lashed out at me, hitting me across the head and stunning me, sending me staggering backwards in a daze before she lunged at me again, and this time she pushed me to the floor, before she slammed her front door shut. Then, as I went to get back up, she showed me the knife and told me that my life, and the life of my daughter, depended on me complying with what she told me to do next.

The pain and the residual shock that came from the blow to the head I suffered, as well as the fact I was fearful she was going to kill me and then Ellie, made me stay where I was, at least until Julia had told me to sit by the radiator. Then she had tied me to it as I had begged to know what was going on.

Not much has happened since then, besides me being gagged and failing to remove the restraints, and as I watch Julia pacing around in front of me, I am wondering what she will do next. I don't know, but what I do know is that she seems just as frustrated about this situation as I am, and it's clear she doesn't want to have a prisoner here just as much as I don't want to be a prisoner here myself. I get further confirmation of that when she makes a phone call and when it's answered, she launches into a tirade directed towards the person at the other end of the line.

'You were followed, you idiot!' Julia cries as she leaves the room, but such is the volume of her voice, it means that I can still hear her talking, or rather, shouting, despite the distance.

I guess that she must be talking to Kyle because he is the person I followed to get here, and it is further proof, as if I needed it, that she is on his side rather than mine and Ellie's.

'Ellie's mother!' Julia goes on. 'She came to my flat and she saw you. She saw us!'

I'm wondering how Kyle is reacting to this newsflash as whatever carefully constructed plan he has been working on starts to crumble around him.

'You should have been more careful! Why was she following you? What mistake have you made?'

Julia is firing loud questions at Kyle, and I wonder if he has any answers to them or if he is genuinely surprised as to how I got suspicious enough to start following him around town. Maybe he remembers the letter in the mail that I questioned him about, or perhaps he recalls me being on his street unexpectedly yesterday and figures I was already on to him then. Or maybe he has absolutely no idea what is going on. I bet he'll be even more confused when he hears what Julia has to say next.

'She's here. I've got her tied up in the flat!' Julia cries before a brief pause, and then she bursts back into noise again. 'Because I had no choice! She was going to tell Ellie that you were cheating on her, and then our plan would have been ruined!'

Our plan?

I get chills from those two words, so I start wriggling my restraints and desperately trying to free myself before Julia can come back into the room and catch me, but she returns a moment later, still holding the phone to her ear. But for some reason, she is no longer angry or frustrated. Unnervingly, she looks quite pleased about something. Then, after telling Kyle to hurry up and finish this so they can both get out of this two-bit town, she says she will see him soon before she hangs up. Then she puts her phone down on the table before looking at me and smiling.

'You were close, but it's too late,' Julia says to me calmly. 'Ellie is doing what we need her to do, and there is nothing you can do to stop it. But try not to worry, this will all be over soon.'

With that, Julia takes a seat at the table and chuckles to herself, leaving me to fear that my daughter is in trouble, and there is absolutely nothing I can do to help her.

22

ELLIE

My mum always tells me that she remembers a time when high street banks were busy places, and everybody in town would queue up at various points of the week to withdraw cash, pay in cheques or even simply just ask for the current balance on their account. But it's hard to imagine that these days as I enter the only bank on the high street that is still open, all the others having closed years ago after the rapid rise of digital banking and less cash in society has made many of them obsolete.

At least the good news is that I don't have to spend too long standing in a queue here because there isn't one, or at least not much of one anyway. There is an elderly woman standing at the counter talking to a clerk but other than that, I'm the only one in here, which means this hopefully won't take too long, and I will be able to call Kyle with the good news when I'm done.

As I wait to be seen, I almost shudder when I recall a time, at least a decade ago now, when, still very young and having no idea what I really wanted to do with my life, Mum suggested I apply for a job in a bank because that had always been a safe, steady career choice. It sure doesn't look that way anymore, and I wonder how long it will be until the clerk behind this counter is out of a job, along with all the other clerks who have already vanished from the high street.

That was one bit of Mum's advice I seem to have done well not to follow.

I smirk to myself at that thought because there haven't been many occasions where I have been right and Mum has been wrong, and as the customer in front of me finishes what she came here to do and moves away from the counter, I step forward and keep smiling as the clerk asks me what he can do to help.

'I'd like to talk to somebody about taking out a loan, please,' I say. 'I called ahead about an hour ago and was told somebody would be happy to speak to me about it.'

'Ahh yes, no problem at all,' the clerk says, and he gets up from his seat before disappearing into a back room. When he returns, he tells me the manager will be with me shortly. I thank him before checking the time and seeing that I still have fifty minutes left on my lunch hour, so I'm hoping that will be enough. I know Kyle is eager to hear from me as well, and will be checking his phone for news, and hopefully, this manager is as helpful as his clerk.

It turns out that he is because after being warmly welcomed by him and offered a cup of coffee, I am taken into a meeting room, and we get down to business. The application for a loan is a fairly straightforward one, and having been a customer at this bank for such a long time, my financial history is clear for the manager to see. He asks why I need the loan, so I give him the reason Kyle suggested I give, which is that I'm looking to upgrade my car, take a holiday and potentially start my own business, and while it seems like an awful lot of money, much of the risk can be offset by my excellent credit rating, the savings I have from my late father, the fact I have steady employment and can make the regular payments and also that I have no current debt at all. The manager can see all that and is aware that I have never mishandled money in any way before, and that's why the application goes well right up until the point when the manager suddenly looks rather serious.

'It's part of my duty here to ask you if your request for money here today is in any way part of a fraudulent scam or scheme.'

'What? No, of course not.'

'Have you been coerced and put under any undue pressure into taking out this loan by another person?'

I don't consider myself as being coerced, so I say no to that one too. Kyle hasn't put me under pressure to do this; it was my suggestion, and he actually turned down my offer before I repeated it and he agreed.

'Are you absolutely certain that your reasons for taking out this loan are genuine and honest?' I am asked then, and while it's clearly a box-ticking exercise from the manager, who is simply following procedure should he ever be questioned about this at a later date, I tell him that I am happy to go ahead. I suppose it's a good thing that they ask such questions because I'm sure they have had a few customers over the years who have been scammed. I've read horror stories in the news about elderly victims falling prey to unscrupulous individuals who have tricked them out of their life savings or had them take out loans before disappearing with the money. It's awful, but I'm aware things like that happen, although this is very different. I've not been talked into doing something by some dodgy builder, unsavoury family member or deceiving friend; I'm doing this to help my husband.

For richer, for poorer.

Right now, we are poorer.

But one stroke of this manager's pen and we are about to be a whole lot richer.

'Last but not least, I have to remind you that you are legally obligated to make payments on this loan at the dates specified in this contract,' he says. 'Failure to do so can result not only in financial penalties but, potentially, prosecution should the loan or the reasons for taking the loan be brought into dispute.'

I swallow hard before saying that I agree because I have technically told a fib about what the money is for. But it's fine because we're going to pay it all back very soon, once Kyle's client pays their money, and then the business will be thriving again.

As I accept the pen from the manager and go to sign, I'm more excited than nervous. I'm excited because I feel like I'm being a good wife. I could have let Daryl ruin my life and leave me a paranoid, untrusting woman who shied away from other men and happy relationships forever, but this right here proves that I haven't let him taint me. I am capable of trust and love and so much more, and as I sign the contract, the manager seems pleased, as am I.

As we conclude our meeting, I am wondering if the reason for the manager's apparent happiness is because it's not often they get this kind of custom on a weekday afternoon anymore. The need for high street banks might be diminishing, but people taking out loans like this one will help keep them alive, thanks to the healthy interest rates on them.

'The money will be in your account by this time tomorrow,' the manager tells me as we shake hands, and I thank him for all his assistance before leaving. No sooner have I got outside then I take out my phone and call Kyle to give him the good news.

'Is it done?' he asks me as he answers, and I confirm that it is.

'Thank you so much. You're a lifesaver!' he tells me, and I smile because I can hear how relieved he is.

I check the time then and realise I'm due back at work in two minutes, so I tell Kyle that I better get a hurry on and will chat to him later. But before I hang up, I mention that I might call around at Mum's place on the way home and see her because we haven't had a catch-up for a few days now.

'Do you have to go tonight? I was thinking we could go out for a drink or two. Celebrate the fact you have just helped save my business and toast to better days ahead.'

Kyle's suggestion is a nice one, and the prospect of champagne and a lovely evening with my husband easily trumps going around to Mum's for a cup of tea, so I agree. He tells me the time and place to meet, and I say that I will see him there before I return to the office to get the rest of my working day over with.

Thankfully, time goes quickly, no doubt helped by the fact that Kyle sends me lots of messages telling me how amazing I am and how he'll never forget that I have helped him so much. In amongst those texts, I send Mum a message asking how her day is, though by the time I've finished work, she hasn't replied. I'm guessing she's busy but so am I, and after hurrying away from my office and into the bar where Kyle wanted to meet tonight, I find my husband already seated at a table with a bottle of champagne on ice.

'Here she is! My amazing wife!' he says as he comes out from behind the table to greet me, and he gives me a big hug as we embrace.

As we take our seats and Kyle pours me a glass, he tells me he loves me, and when we toast, we toast to an exciting future, and it's one that sounds even better when Kyle drops a very large hint about the two of us one day making this a family of three.

I feel like I couldn't be happier as I sip my champagne, and as the bubbles go straight to my head, I am glowing in this fuzzy bubble of contentment. But even amidst that, I pause for a moment to think of Mum, who still hasn't messaged me back yet. But it's not so much her not doing that which troubles me, rather the fact that I am here toasting to the good life with my amazing man while she has endured so much struggle and suffering in her life.

'I wish Mum could have this,' I say, looking around the bar. 'Champagne on a weeknight. A nice holiday. Somebody to wine and dine her. She deserves to be as happy as I am right now.'

Kyle understands and agrees before I go on.

'I've been thinking,' I say to my husband as he pours himself another glass of bubbly. 'Once we have everything sorted out with the business and things are going well, maybe, one day, we could give my mum some money, and she might be able to retire a little earlier?'

Kyle doesn't say anything to that but is clearly listening, so I carry on.

'It's just that she's always worked so hard to support me. All those years of long shifts at the supermarket. I feel like it's enough. She deserves a break or at least to do something less demanding on her body. Maybe you could hire her to your business once it's grown? She could do some admin work or accounts or something. We could pay her a nice wage, and she could maybe get to enjoy herself like we are doing a little more too. What do you think?'

Kyle ponders it for a moment before smiling.

'I think that's a great idea,' he says. 'And I think your mother is very lucky to have you as a daughter.'

'I just want to pay her back for all the sacrifices she made for me,' I insist. 'And, of course, I wouldn't be here now if it wasn't for her saving me from Daryl.'

Maybe it's the champagne but I'm suddenly feeling a little teary, which is why Kyle reaches out and takes my hand before giving it a squeeze.

'You and your mum are incredible, and I'll be happy to help her out as soon as I can,' he says before proposing another toast.

As I raise my glass, he raises his and beams at me.

'To us!' he says, smiling widely. 'And to your mum!'

23

DAWN

'Cheers.'

That's the unnecessary comment from Julia as she raises a glass of red wine in my direction before taking a long glug.

My captor is sitting at the table in front of me and is now drinking from the bottle of wine she opened, as if she's so calm and relaxed that there's no reason not to partake in a little alcohol this evening. I know it's the evening now because I can see the sun has set on the other side of the windows, which means I have been tied up here all day.

Is anybody missing me? Ellie, perhaps. One of my friends, maybe? They might have messaged or called to see how I am. But they'll probably just presume I'm busy and will get back to them soon.

Will I ever get the chance to do that?

Or am I stuck here forever?

As I watch Julia consume more wine, I get the sense that rather than revelling in my misfortune, she is actually just bored and simply drinking to entertain herself and pass the time. Having heard her talking to Kyle on the phone earlier and after she then told me that this would be over soon, I am guessing she is waiting for him to come back here, and then things can progress, though what that means for me and Ellie, I have no idea.

I try to speak again, but my voice is still muffled by my gag, though I do at least regain Julia's attention after she has poured herself another glass.

'So I suppose you are wondering what all this is about,' she says to me as she runs a finger around the rim of her glass, picking up a few droplets of wine on her digit before licking them off. 'You must have so many questions? Who am I? Who is Kyle? What do we want? Why did we target you and your daughter?'

Julia chuckles to herself and takes another swig, and I can clearly see that she intends to drink that whole bottle, although if she wants to get drunk and potentially sloppy, that's fine by me.

'Don't worry, you're not the first people we've done this to,' Julia says smugly. 'You might be thinking you're special but you're not. We run long cons, tricking people over several months. Kyle and I have done this to plenty of other people before, although I will admit you are the only one who has come close to stopping us before we achieved our aims.'

Julia almost seems to be giving me a little bit of respect there, although respect might not be the right word as she stares down at me like some wounded animal chained up in her home while she indulges in her favourite drink.

'Kyle and I take it in turns to seduce somebody,' she goes on. 'I did it last time, and now he's done it to Ellie. What we do is, we make that person fall in love with us to the point where they will do something stupid. Something like give up their savings to us or, in Ellie's case, take out a sizeable bank loan which we can then disappear with and never pay back.'

A bank loan?

'You're wondering what I mean by a loan, aren't you?' Julia says, and if it wasn't frustrating enough that she has me tied up here, it's even more frustrating that she is so easily able to read my mind.

'Earlier today, your daughter took out a loan for £100,000,' Julia says with a satisfied smile. 'She did that because she believes the money is to help her husband's business get through a few cash-flow problems. Mainly, she did it because she is a loyal, loving wife, or at least she thinks she is. But she's simply nothing more than a fool, and you know what they say about fools and money. They're easily parted.'

I cannot believe what I'm hearing. Ellie has taken a loan out for 100k. *Is she crazy?*

I try to speak again, but Julia just sighs before carrying on.

'Once the money is in Ellie's account, which should be by lunchtime tomorrow, she will send it to the account Kyle tells her to send it to, and then that will be it. We'll have the money, and we will be gone, never to be seen again, while your daughter will be the one left owing the bank a small fortune. Simple, right?'

I bite into my gag as I try to suppress my anger at what I'm hearing.

'Then we'll spend a good portion of the money having a great time travelling and living like kings and queens until we find ourselves another target. It'll be my turn then to do what Kyle just did, and I can't wait because that's always the fun part. It's not as much fun to be the one sitting around waiting for the other one to finish the job.'

Julia is definitely bored and has just confirmed it, and I'm wondering if I can use that against her. But before I can, she speaks again.

'Everything you think you know about Kyle is an illusion,' she says. 'You were already starting to figure that out yourself, which means Kyle got sloppy, and I will have to speak to him about that. Although I made a mistake too. That letter that came to your house with my name on. It should have come here. I accidentally put in the wrong address while I was drunk one night. Ooops.'

Julia looks at her wine and shrugs.

'But even so, you still don't know the half of it, just like Ellie has no clue either. If she did, she certainly wouldn't be sitting in a bar sipping champagne with him right now and toasting to their future together.'

Julia laughs as she gets up from her seat and walks over to me before she shows me the photo on her phone. When she does, I see an image of Ellie smiling as she holds a glass of champagne, and while she looks as happy as I ever recall seeing her, it's only because she has no idea that she is being tricked.

'Doesn't she look sweet,' Julia says. 'She really is rather pretty, actually.'

Julia shrugs before putting her phone back in her pocket, but before she can walk away from me again, I start making as much noise as I can to indicate that I desperately have something to say.

Perhaps her judgement is clouded slightly by the wine she has consumed since she started enlightening me about her and Kyle's devious plan, but to my relief, Julia willingly removes my gag, though not before telling me that if I scream, it will go back on again and never come off.

But I don't plan on screaming, not just because I know it's futile, but also because I genuinely do have something to say. I have questions, lots of them, and I need answers, if only so that one day, I might be able to explain things to Ellie when she desperately wants to know how and why this could have happened to her.

'I don't understand how you think you can get away with this,' I say, my throat dry and hoarse from straining it so much and from lack of water. 'Kyle and Ellie are married. He can't just vanish.'

'Are they?'

I don't like the way Julia seems so smug when she said that.

'What do you mean?' I cry. 'Yes, they got married! I was at the wedding! They're husband and wife, which means he can't just run away and disappear. They're legally bound. The police will track him down.'

'No, they won't because they don't know his real name, just like they don't know my real name either. Do you really think I'm called Julia and he's called Kyle? They are just aliases. Fictitious names that we embody for a while but actually mean nothing.'

'But how did Kyle marry Ellie with a fake name? I don't understand,' I say, unable to get my head around all this.

'Oh, Dawn, the wedding wasn't legal. It was all a charade.'

'What?'

'Why do you think Kyle suggested they have it overseas rather than in England. Not because it was cheaper - it's because it's much easier there to get away with what we did. Yes, it was a nice ceremony, and vows were exchanged but not legally binding ones, at least not in Turkey anyway. Ellie and Kyle aren't really husband and wife; it's all a sham.'

'But what about the guests Kyle had at the wedding?'

'They were all just acting. Kyle paid a few tourists a hundred euros each to show up and pretend. Easy.'

The full horror of the situation is starting to dawn on me now, and I'm no longer worrying about the financial impact of this on my daughter. I'm worried about the emotional one because how the hell is she going to react when she learns that her beautiful wedding day was nothing more than a charade? There is being lied to and then there is that, and I fear my daughter may never recover from such a betrayal ever again.

What else is a lie?

'Does he even have a business?' I ask next, referring to the story he has spun us about him being involved in logistics.

'He does but certainly not the one he told you about,' Julia says with a smirk. 'His business, and mine, is scamming naïve people like your daughter. Any time he has been on the phone pretending to be talking to customers, he's really been talking to me and giving me updates.'

'You bitch,' I say, my voice dripping with venom. 'I'll kill you and him. I'll kill both of you for this.'

I might sound like I'm overexaggerating slightly, but in this moment right here, I mean every word of it.

'Yeah, yeah, yeah. Whatever,' Julia says with a shake of her head, looking as bored of me as she is of having to be in this flat while Kyle is out there having fun.

Looking around the flat, I try to figure out how all this works, and once again, Julia seems to pre-empt my thoughts and fills in the blanks for me.

'This is just a cheap place we rent as a base,' she says. 'The main house that Kyle has is a rental, but we paid in cash and obviously used fake identification there. The idea was for him to present as a successful businessman so that Ellie would not doubt him when he said he was just going through a few money troubles after their *marriage*.'

Julia makes sure to stress that last word to emphasise it was not a marriage at all.

'It's a surprisingly simple con, and like I say, between the two of us, we have done this to plenty of people over the years,' she goes on. 'I estimate we've made over a million pounds in total from our various scams, which is quite an achievement, although we both have expensive taste and spend it almost as quickly as it comes in.'

Julia walks back to the table and picks up the bottle on it before telling me that her beverage of choice this evening cost her over a hundred pounds, though she then goes on to remind me that with the windfall coming her way tomorrow, money is not an issue.

It's all dark and depressing for me to hear, and I feel on the verge of tears, though if I do cry, I'll be weeping for my daughter more than me. But before I give in to my emotions and end up giving Julia even more satisfaction, I take a shot at ruining her mood and try and make her second guess her and her partner's decision to target my poor Ellie.

'You know, you're not the first two people to mess with me and my daughter,' I say defiantly. 'There was another pair before you. A father and son, and things didn't work out well for them in the end. One of them is dead and the other went to prison, and believe me when I say that when this is over, one of those two things will have happened to you.'

I expect my words to have some kind of an impact on Julia, or at least I'm hoping they do. That's why I'm disappointed when the woman standing in front of me simply retakes her seat and picks up the wine bottle again before explaining why she isn't worried.

'You won't kill us because you won't get the chance to,' she says rather simply. 'And if, for whatever reason, Kyle or I end up in prison one day for our crimes then that will be a shame. But do you know what the cool thing about prison is? They let almost everybody out of there again in the end.'

As Julia drinks, I think about how she is right, and I hate it.

They do let people out, people who have done even worse things than she has.

People like Harvey.

24

HARVEY

There have been many moments on this journey when I have feared it might not end in the way I want it to. Like the moment when the van was inching along in the queue to get onto the ferry, and I feared the vehicle would be selected for a random search, a search that would result in me and my fellow stowaway behind all these fridges being discovered and promptly detained, along with the driver, who would probably pretend that he had no idea we had hitched a ride with him. Or like the moment when I figured we had made it onto the ferry because we were swaying, and I could hear the roar of the boat's engines below us, along with the voices of security guards who seemed to be conducting a sweep of the vehicle bay during the journey. But most of all, I feared being caught when the boat stopped and the van was moving again because I could clearly hear the voices of customs officials outside the vehicle questioning our driver as to his reason for being in the UK today.

Hearing that we had arrived in England was exciting, but it was also nerve-wracking as I listened to the driver explain that he was simply delivering refrigerators to a client on behalf of his employer. I presumed he had falsified paperwork to back this claim up, and he must have had something because the customs officials I could hear outside eventually stopped questioning him and allowed him to be on his way.

As the van moved on, leaving the ferry behind and officially entering England, the stowaway beside me hadn't been able to contain his excitement, and I knew why.

Despite the driver smuggling us into this country making it clear to us both that we had to stay quiet throughout the journey, the man hiding in the back of this van with me has spoken a few times, even when I've reminded him to shut up. He told me his name, which is Grigor, and he told me about the town he was from, although I've already forgotten the name of that because it didn't seem important. His reason for fleeing his homeland and trying to get to England wasn't particularly important for me to learn either, but he told me that, saying he had got in trouble with some bad people and needed to leave before they came after him.

At one point, Grigor asked me for my reason for going to England in such an illegal and secretive manner, but I simply shook my head and stayed quiet, not just because I didn't want anybody to overhear us talking, but because it was none of his business. This is a personal mission for me, and nobody needs to know about it, which is the way it has stayed so far, and it seems to be working.

We've been driving for a while since we got off the boat, and I'm wondering if we are ever going to stop and be allowed out. It gets so bad that at one point, Grigor, the annoying passenger that he is, starts worrying that we have been tricked and that we are going to end up enslaved under the control of the kinds of bad people he was trying to evade back home. I don't have the patience to listen to his worries, though I do have the time because there's not much else I can do, so I'm bracing myself to listen to his chattering for a while longer when the van suddenly stops.

Grigor immediately falls silent, and we both listen out as we hear the engine disengage before a door opens and then slams shut. Then we both hear the footsteps that make their way around to the rear of the van, and as the two of us peer through the darkness towards those back doors, we are not quite sure what we are going to see when they open.

When they do open, the van isn't exactly flooded with light because it's dark outside, although we still both squint as our eyes adjust to the sudden change.

'Get out,' comes the gruff instruction from the driver, and Grigor and I share a look before we do as we are told, clambering over the fridges that block our path to the doors before we jump out of the back of the van. When our feet hit the ground, they are landing on English soil, a fact confirmed when I ask exactly where we are now.

'You're about twenty miles outside of Felixstowe,' the driver says as he closes the doors to the van, and he already looks like he is ready to get back behind the wheel and drive away.

'What do we do now?' Grigor asks nervously as he looks around at the dark, deserted country road we are on.

'Whatever you want,' the driver says before he does exactly what I assumed he was going to do and gets back in the van before starting the engine and moving away.

Grigor calls after him, as if expecting a better service than this, but I don't care because this is fine by me. I know Felixstowe is in Suffolk, which is the same county Dawn and Ellie live in, so I'm not a million miles away from them now.

Looking ahead, I see a road sign that tells me the next town is five miles from here, so I set off walking in that direction, and now Grigor is asking me where I am going.

'Get lost and enjoy England,' I say to him as I don't look back, pacing away and hoping that at some point along my route, I might encounter another vehicle operated by a driver who is willing to give me a lift to get me closer to my final destination.

But it's not a problem if that doesn't happen because I'll walk all the way there if I have to.

I'll walk right through the night to get to where I need to be.

Before dawn, I hope to see the woman with that same name, and I'll see her daughter too.

Not a damn thing can stop me now.

25

ELLIE

I've drunk far too much champagne for a work night, and I know I'll pay for it in the morning when I wake up with a sore head and a dry throat. But it's always better to live for today rather than tomorrow, or at least that's what I tell myself as Kyle and I get out of the taxi that has just dropped us off at home.

No sooner have I got out then I almost stumble and trip, but fortunately, my husband has better balance than I do and grabs my arm before I can hit the concrete. The taxi drives off as I thank my man for catching me, and Kyle simply gives me a wink before taking out the house keys from his pocket. But to prove that he is not totally immune from the effects of all the alcohol we have guzzled this evening, he ends up dropping the keys on the ground and has to then resort to very gingerly kneeling down to pick them back up again.

'Look at the state of us,' I say, laughing a little too loudly and possibly drawing the ire of a few of our neighbours who are most likely already in bed. But I can't help it. Controlling the volume of my voice has never been easy when I've had a drink, and as I cheer loudly after Kyle successfully retrieves the keys from the pavement, I see a curtain twitching in the window of a house across the road.

Instead of shutting up and shyly going inside as quickly as I can, I wave emphatically at the neighbour who is checking outside to see what all the commotion is before Kyle, giggling, tells me to stop it and get in the house.

'Hmmm, is that my big, strong man bossing me around?' I purr as I reach out and pull Kyle towards me before planting a big kiss on his lips. While my eyes are closed initially, I make sure to open one of them and take a peek at the house across the street to see if we're still being watched. We're not, which is probably for the best, though it would have been funny if we were, at least to me, anyway.

We pass by Kyle's car on the driveway as we stagger towards the front door, my husband having left his vehicle here and taken a taxi into town to meet me. As for my car, it's back at the office, and I seem to be making a habit lately of leaving my vehicle at work so I can go out drinking afterwards.

I briefly consider going on some kind of detox, starting 'next Monday' of course, like every good diet does, but before I can worry about that, I just need to get inside, as does my husband, who currently looks like he is trying to remember how to use a door key.

Kyle takes longer than he should to get the key in the lock, but he finally manages it, not helped by me pinching his behind and whispering silly things in his ear as he works, and then we are officially home. But no sooner have we got through the front door then my lips are back on my husband's, and this time, I am not going to allow him to break away.

Fuelled by a powerful combination of the champagne, the huge loan I took out today and all the exciting things Kyle and I have spent the evening talking about doing in the future, I drag my husband into the bedroom before we make love.

It's far more intense than it's ever been before, and Kyle seems much more engaged with me than he has ever been, as if he's enjoying my body for the first time. It certainly won't be the last time, but once is more than enough for one night, and as the pair of us lie back on the bed beside each other, breathless and buoyant, we both agree that was a lot of fun.

'We need to drink champagne more often,' I say, and Kyle agrees before I joke that rather than put the loan I took out straight into his business, we should just go to the airport and fly away and spend the money somewhere warm and sunny without worrying about ever paying it back.

It's a joke, of course, but Kyle doesn't find it quite as funny as I hoped he would, and I get the sense something might be wrong as he gets up off the bed and goes into the bathroom.

'Is everything okay?' I ask him, getting up myself and following him in after I have put on a dressing gown to replace all the clothes I hurriedly threw off not so long ago.

'Yeah, fine,' Kyle says as he puts toothpaste on his toothbrush and turns the tap on. 'Do you want to check your bank account? See if the money's gone in yet?'

'It won't have. They said it would be tomorrow.'

'I know, but it might be quicker. No harm in checking,' he says before he puts the brush in his mouth and starts washing away some of the remnants of the wine he consumed.

I figure it can't hurt to spend ten seconds checking, so I grab my phone from my handbag and open my mobile banking app, though when I do, I see that the money has not gone in there yet, as I suspected.

'Nope. It's not there,' I say, and Kyle nods before spitting out some water and brushing again.

'Patience, dear hubs,' I say with a grin before I leave the bathroom and flop onto the bed, my phone still in my hand because I want to make a check on my messages. But when I do, I see that Mum still hasn't replied to me and considering how late it is, I doubt she is going to do so now.

'Hmmm, that's weird,' I say as Kyle re-enters the bedroom.

'What is?' he asks as he pulls on a scruffy t-shirt in preparation for bed.

'Mum still hasn't messaged me back. Do you think she's okay?'

'I'm sure she's fine. Maybe she hasn't seen it.'

'Yeah, I don't think she has,' I say as I check the message and see that while it has been delivered, it has not been opened and read by the recipient. 'I wonder if she's lost her phone somewhere.'

'Possibly. Has she lost it before?'

'No, I don't think so. She's usually good at looking after things.'

'You mean, she's not as bad as you?' Kyle teases, and I roll my eyes as he joins me on the bed.

'Put your phone down, and let's get some sleep,' he suggests, and that does sound like a good idea, so I follow his word, and the pair of us get under the duvet together.

As he turns off the bedside lamp, I put my phone on charge, though I make sure it's not on silent, just in case Mum does message or call me at some point in the night, telling me that something is wrong. It's funny because it's usually the parent who would be anxiously listening out for their child to know they are okay, but the roles are reversed here, though it's not totally weird because as I get older, I find myself worrying about Mum far more than I ever did when I was young. But what is weird is that she hasn't read my message, and even as Kyle snuggles into me and wishes me a good night's sleep, I am unable to relax.

'I wish I wasn't drunk,' I say, and Kyle asks me why.

'So I could drive over to Mum's and check she is okay,' I say before I pick up my phone. 'Maybe I'll just call her and see if she answers.'

I go to do that, but Kyle stops me.

'Don't be silly. It's very late, and she's probably asleep. Or maybe she has taken an extra shift at the supermarket. She sometimes does nights, right? That might explain why she hasn't looked at her phone. She's busy working.'

'Maybe,' I say, but even though that would explain it, I almost hope Mum isn't working overtime because it would only prove that she is still struggling for money, and I'd hate for that to be the case. I told her not to spend a fortune on her dress for my wedding, but she didn't listen, and while it was a lovely dress, surely it wasn't worth it if she has to work non-stop to pay it off now.

'Sleep well,' Kyle says before rolling over, and I roll over too, trying to do just that. But before I drift off, there is enough time for one more quick, paranoid search on the internet to see if there are any more articles about Harvey.

There are not.

Is that a good thing?

I guess so.

Nothing to worry about there.

Nothing to worry about with Mum either.

At least I hope so.

26

DAWN

It must be very late now - the middle of the night, I presume - and it's a time when most people are asleep. I know Julia is because I can hear her snores filtering in from the bedroom, her heavy breathing during sleep perhaps a consequence of that full bottle of red wine she had to herself before going to bed. But I'm wide awake and know that there is little chance of sleep, not just because I'm very uncomfortable positioned on the floor of this flat with my hands tied and my mouth gagged, but because I simply cannot rest without knowing that Ellie is ok.

She must be with Kyle now, probably sleeping soundly beside him and enjoying the love and warmth that comes from being alongside your life partner during the night. I bet she is sleeping blissfully, totally unaware of the huge problem that exists in her life, as well as all the sadness and pain that is to come. There's a part of me that almost wishes that my daughter didn't have to wake up because if she didn't then she wouldn't have to find out that Kyle lied to her; he has left her in a horrible financial mess, and she isn't even married, despite walking down an aisle in a white dress and saying several vows.

What a mess.

Oh, Ellie, how could this have happened?

While I don't blame my daughter for being misled by a charming, attractive man like Kyle, who is clearly a very clever and calculating person with a lie for every occasion, I do blame her for her foolishness in taking out such a big loan for him. I can't believe the bank agreed to give her so much money either but more than that, I can't believe that she was stupid enough to think that the best thing to do was to go and sign herself up for a load of debt simply on the word of another person. Sure, she trusts Kyle and thinks he is in love with her, but she shouldn't have been so blinded by that love as to commit to such a monetary burden as she has done. Now, Kyle and his despicable partner in crime are going to run away tomorrow as soon as they get their hands on that money, and there is seemingly nothing I or my daughter can do about it.

Before retiring to bed, a tipsy Julia told me what would happen when they had the money and were preparing to leave. She said they would leave me tied up until they had gotten far enough away before Kyle would message Ellie and tell her where I was, allowing me to be rescued. It would be the last message Kyle ever sent her before he disposed of his phone and vanished alongside Julia, never to be seen again, at least not by us anyway. But they would resurface at some point, many miles away from this town most likely, and when they did, they would look to take money from some other poor soul.

So now, by my calculations, my daughter has dated both a murderer and a con artist.

Wow, Ellie, you really know how to pick them.

I would cry if I didn't start laughing then, the dark humour of the situation getting to me and leaving me shaking my head in disbelief as I sit here in the gloomy living area of this flat, wondering how many hours it is until the sun rises and the lives of me and my daughter get even worse.

But as I look around at the environment I am trapped in, a thought occurs to me that hadn't before. I see the chair that Julia was sitting on, and it's beside the table upon which sits the empty bottle of wine.

My best chance of escaping is if I could cut through my restraints, and the glass wine bottle might just do it.

But I'd need to break the glass to create sharp shards and then get my hands on one of the jagged pieces.

How do I do that?

Reaching out with my left leg, I stretch the limb as far as I can and when I do, I see that the end of my foot can just about touch the chair. Taking another few seconds to try and visualise the plan in my mind, I have an idea, and while I doubt I am lucky enough for it to actually work, it is the only thing I can try in my situation.

What if I was to kick the chair into the table and cause the wine bottle to topple over and fall to the floor?

If I did that, the bottle would surely smash as soon as it hit the hard floor, and then I might be able to scrape one of the shards of glass over to me with my feet before potentially getting to the point where I could possibly get it into my hands and use it to cut through the tie around my wrists.

One big problem - even if that somehow worked - would be that the bottle would make a loud noise when it smashed and would be likely to wake up Julia, who would come racing into this room, see what I had done and stop me before I could get any further. But what else can I try? I can't think of any other way I can get out of this, and if this is the only chance I have at stopping these people before they escape after ruining Ellie's life then I have to take it.

Here goes nothing.

Kicking the leg of the chair, I watch as it hits the table, and immediately, the wine bottle starts wobbling.

'Come on,' I say under my breath, willing gravity to take over and play its part, and that's exactly what happens as the bottle falls onto its side before rolling along the table.

I brace myself for the loud noise that is about to occur, and sure enough, the sound of the glass hitting the floor is incredibly loud in this otherwise silent flat. But it's too late to worry about that now, and I quickly get to work trying to scrape one of the bigger shards of glass towards me.

There are plenty to choose from because the wine bottle really has made a mess, sending out pieces in all directions and covering the floor, and if I am able to get out of here, I'll have to be careful not to cut myself on the way. But I'm not free yet, though I am able to manoeuvre a sizeable shard of glass to a position where it is now right beside me.

Manoeuvring and contorting my body, I nudge the shard with my upper thigh to the point where it is almost behind me. Then, groaning as I strain my body, I get it to a place where my fingers can touch it.

Finally, after more struggling, I pick the piece of glass up, and then I can make a start on trying to use it to cut through the tie.

The first thing that ends up being cut is my skin, and blood quickly pours from my palm as the shard cuts into me almost as much as the ties, but I refuse to slow down, working desperately because I know Julia might be awake now and about to come in here at any second and put a stop to my defiant plan.

'Come on,' I say desperately, my voice louder now than the last time I uttered those words, but I can see that the glass is doing its job, and my restraints are weakening.

Then they suddenly snap, and I can't believe it.

I'm free!

Getting to my feet as quickly as I can, I pull out my mouth gag before I make a quick check on my palm to assess the damage to my hand from the glass. But while it's bloody, it's just a flesh wound and the least of my problems. I just need to get out of here as quickly as I can before I meet any further obstacles.

I'm glad I'm still wearing my shoes because one obstacle could have been the glass that litters the floor between me and the doorway, but I'm just about to easily step over all the shards and run out of the room when disaster strikes.

Julia is awake, and she has just walked in.

She's as shocked to see me standing up as I am to see her in the doorway blocking my exit route, and for a second, neither one of us speaks as our respective minds search for a next move. But then Julia springs into action first, rushing towards me and clearly fancying her chances of overpowering me if it comes to a tussle. But no sooner has she run towards me then she lets out a huge shriek of pain before falling to the floor, and when I look down at her, I see exactly what she has done.

She's just stepped on all that broken glass with her bare feet.

I didn't need to hear her shriek or see all the blood that is now coming from the soles of her feet to appreciate how painful that must have been for her, but while she is temporarily trying to recover from that, I spring into action.

But I'm not just running for the door because while I might be able to escape easily, it's no good now that Julia is awake and aware that I've gone because she could then contact Kyle and tell him their plan is under threat again. I also don't like the thought of her potentially chasing after me, so that's why I decide to make sure she can't do either of those things.

Grabbing her by her hair, I pull her towards the same radiator she had me tied to before I wrap the tea towel in her mouth to silence her screams, just like she did to me. Then I start wrapping one of the pieces of the tie around her wrists, and while she tries to hit me and slow me down, I'm angry and determined enough to not let her defeat me.

Adrenaline is a powerful thing, and it's certainly the thing that is fuelling me as I restrain Julia, turning the captor into the prisoner, and once she is tied up, I make sure to kick away all the shards of glass so they are far enough away from her so that she can't escape by the same means I did.

'Come back here!' Julia screams at me as I leave the room, but I have no intention of doing that, though I'm not quite heading for the door just yet. I go into the bedroom and find Julia's phone and make sure to take that with me, just so she can't call Kyle and warn him, if she is somehow able to get free. I find my phone too, and see a message on there from Ellie that was sent several hours ago, though she'll understand why I haven't messaged her back yet very shortly.

As I take one last look at Julia, I see the fear and frustration in her face, but it's a sight to behold after all the satisfaction she gained from telling me about her sordid little plot earlier. I see her struggling but not getting very far, but even if she does get free, she might chase after me, but with the injuries to her feet, I doubt she will get anywhere fast.

With that, I make my exit, running out of the door and onto the street, where I find my car still waiting for me where I left it. Then I hop in behind the wheel and start the engine before speeding away as quickly as I can, glad that the empty streets at this late hour will help me get to where I am going as quickly as possible.

I need to get to my daughter's place.

But I plan on taking backup with me.

It's time to get the police involved.

It's time to end this.

27

HARVEY

While walking through the night to get to Dawn's house might have been a plan I was happy enough to go along with as long as it got me there, plans change, and there's no point not taking a better opportunity if it comes along. That's what I did when a car pulled up alongside me and the male driver asked me where I was going.

He was clearly a little surprised to see somebody out walking at such a late hour, especially because a little rain had started to fall, and he asked me if I was okay. I told him that I was, not looking to make much of a fuss, but rather than drive on and leave me to whatever I was doing, the driver offered to give me a lift.

I saw that he had taxi markings on his vehicle and initially presumed that he was wanting to make a little money from me, but he quickly pre-empted that by saying the fare would be free because he had already finished his shift and was simply heading in the same direction as me as he made his way home. Then he asked me where I was going specifically, and I gave him the name of the town Dawn and Ellie reside in, figuring it was best to give a more general destination rather than their exact residential address, just in case he recognised it from all the media reports back when it was big news.

'I can take you there if you like?' the driver offered then before telling me that it wouldn't be that far out of his way, and he would be more than happy to have a little company for the last part of his drive.

While I was considering whether or not to accept the kind offer, I thought about how it can sometimes be a bad idea for a person to accept a ride with a total stranger, especially in the circumstances I had found myself in, at a dark roadside in the middle of nowhere. There are all sorts of stories about hitchhikers getting into a vehicle with somebody who appears to be friendly but then turns out to be very dangerous, and the next thing that happens, a dog walker is finding a dead body at the side of the road - the dead hitchhiker, murdered for simply trusting somebody they should not have.

Did I really want to risk something like that happening to me? Of course not, but then I thought about how, in this example, there was very little chance the driver was going to turn out to be more dangerous than I was. In my case, it would be the driver who was unwittingly putting himself in a perilous position because I was already a killer myself, and I was on my way to commit another serious crime, so I felt confident I could take my chances with him. That's why I said yes, and after getting into the front passenger seat alongside him, the kindly driver drove us both on in the direction of Dawn and Ellie's town.

It's been over forty minutes since I was picked up at the roadside and in that time, the driver and I have chatted about various things, ranging from the weather, the pros and cons of the car we were sitting in and the virtues of being up and awake at this time of night while everybody else was sleeping. But we haven't just discussed banal topics for the whole journey; we got deeper than that, much deeper than two men would probably be expected to. Maybe it was the randomness of our meeting, or perhaps it was simply down to the fact that both of us knew we would never see the other one again after tonight, but the pair of us opened up as we drove along the dark country roads.

The driver confessed that he had lost his wife recently, and rather than spend night after night lying beside her empty pillow and reminiscing on what he had lost, he had taken to conducting his shifts as a taxi driver in the evening. He told me he used to work solely in the daytime but found the nights difficult now he had an empty house to go back to so had swapped his working patterns and tended to sleep all day and drive all night. He admitted that he found there was a more peaceful energy when the sun had gone down that he wanted to experience, and while it was clear he was simply doing what he could to get over the grief of becoming a widower, it seemed to be working for him. But it was his honesty that prompted me to mention my own loss too.

Discussing Daryl has never been easy and has rarely been something I've actually done, mainly because it's always been difficult to suppress the rage I feel about the fact my boy's life was ended in such a vicious way as being beaten over the head with a rock by an Englishwoman in a park. But I found it much easier to stay mellow as I discussed my own loss, possibly because of the calming environment of this car or maybe because I knew that every minute that went by, we were another mile or so closer to me getting my revenge on the people who caused it.

I obviously didn't go into any detail about how my son had lost his life because the driver would surely have recognised the news story then. Instead, I kept the details of Daryl's passing vague, though I was much more substantial when I talked about what it felt like to know your child had gone forever.

I talked about the feelings of loss, shame, regret, denial and fear I had experienced, even fighting back a couple of tears at one point and prompting the driver to tell me that things didn't get easier but we get stronger. I appreciated that, and I also appreciated the fact that I was able to spin my tale of woe into a cover story about why I, an American man, had been wandering around sleepy Suffolk at such a strange hour.

I told my driver that after the death of my son, I felt the need for adventure and had taken many trips since then, leading up to this latest one right here, where I had simply come to England and started exploring. The driver absolutely loved that concept and said he understood the need for a grieving person to change their environment, although he admitted he wasn't as brave as me and couldn't see himself going to America and walking around to see where it led him.

I had rather been enjoying our chat as we had driven on, but my ultimate goal refocused in my mind when I saw a road sign for Dawn and Ellie's hometown, and after double-checking if I was happy enough to be dropped off on the high street, I confirmed that I was, and the car came to a stop.

'It was a pleasure to meet you,' the driver says to me as I get out, and I say the same before I am asked what my next plan is.

'I'll just see where life takes me,' I reply with a cheerful smile, and the driver seems to enjoy that answer before he drives away and leaves me alone again at the roadside. I'm sure he wouldn't have enjoyed it so much if he knew what I was actually planning on doing next, but he'll find out soon enough. It'll be all over the news channels and the newspapers within the next twenty-four hours or so, and he'll certainly have a chastising moment when he realises he unwittingly helped a killer get to the scene of his victims much sooner.

Free to roam around a town where all the residents are still tucked up in their beds, I reach into my rucksack and pull out the folded pieces of paper upon which are the Google Map directions instructing me on how to precisely get to Dawn's address. It feels a little old-fashioned to be using printouts from the internet instead of a mobile phone app but not as old-fashioned as an actual map, I suppose.

Looking for road signs and getting my bearings, I eventually figure out which way I need to go, and then I start walking. But just before that, I made sure to double-check on another important part of my toolkit today, and that was why I put my hand on the blade of the knife inside my rucksack. It's still there, easily accessible and ready to be used when I need it.

As I follow my directions, I am aware I'm incredibly close now, but as I near Dawn's street, I pass another place that I wanted to visit while I was here. It's not going to be a pleasant place to stop, but I feel like I have to do it.

Entering the park where my son lost his life, I'm not going to be as morbid as to find the exact spot where Dawn killed him. I'm not quite sure where it is and besides, it's pitch black, and I'd never find it even if I wanted to. But I did want to pause in the general vicinity and take a moment to speak to the spirit of my son, very similar to how I did when I was at his graveside only a few days ago. Maybe this is the best place to do it too, because while that cemetery in LA is where his bones now lie, this park here is where his soul really left his body.

'I'm about to make things right for you, son,' I say out loud, staring at the silhouettes of all the dark trees that surround me and hearing a branch creaking in the breeze. 'Dawn and Ellie will die tonight, and then you can finally be at rest. I'm going to end this. I promise.'

With that, I turn and stride out of the park and back towards the glow of the streetlamps. Another quick check on the paper map in my hand tells me that it should be one more turn of a street corner, and then I'll be at my destination.

My heart is thumping in my chest as I round the corner and see the street sign that bears the name I know so well. This street was reported on in numerous articles, and as I see the row of houses on either side of the road here, I recognise them as the backdrop to the many reporters who stood here and talked live about the crazy events involving two of the residents.

Then I see the house I came to visit.

It's familiar both from the news reports and from all the times I have studied it on Google Street view, getting my bearings online so I would be as comfortable as possible when it came time to stand here in person. But I double-check the number on the door because I can't afford to get the wrong place.

If I'm planning to kill the residents inside, I better make sure I have the right house.

But this is where I need to be, and I quickly move around to the rear of the property, lifting the latch on the side gate and making it into the back garden. Then I try the back door, but it is locked, as expected. However, there is a window nearby, and after locating a suitable object that will shatter glass, I launch a heavy plant pot at that window.

The plant pot shatters the glass before I scramble up and get inside, and once in, my boots crunch across the broken glass on the kitchen floor, and I quickly reach into my rucksack for the knife.

As soon as it is in my grasp, I am on the hunt for anybody inside, heading for the stairs quickly because I expect to find the residents sleeping in their beds up there. I can't wait to see Dawn's face when she sees me entering her bedroom with a deadly weapon, and I will make sure to give her just enough time to scream and beg for mercy before I deliver the brutal blows.

Passing a bathroom, I find an empty bedroom before I see a closed door at the end of the hallway. Dawn must be behind here, and I'm ready for her, the knife lifted above me as I use my free hand to turn the handle and enter quickly.

Then I hit the lights and prepare to lock eyes with the woman who killed my son.

But she is not here.

The bed is empty.

No, this can't be happening.

Rushing around the rest of the house, I desperately try to find her or her daughter, but the place is entirely unoccupied. However, I know I have the right place because of all the family photos that are on display on various walls and mantelpieces. I even see a fridge magnet showing Dawn, Ellie and a person who I assume is Sean.

But it's while I am looking at the magnet that I see something else.

It's a wedding invitation for the marriage of Ellie and a guy called Kyle.

Pulling it off the fridge, I stare at the smiling face of my son's ex-girlfriend before flipping the invite over and reading it. The text on the back mentions a ceremony in Turkey, and judging by the date, it occurred only a few days ago. Is that why Dawn isn't here? Is she in Turkey? Is Ellie there too? If so, what does this mean for my plan?

Then I see the address that people are asked to RSVP to, and I figure that is where Ellie and her new man, Kyle, must live.

Checking the printout of the town map I have with me, I search for the relevant street name before I find it. It looks to be some way from here, but I can start walking and get there soon enough, certainly while it's still dark outside.

I guess that's sorted then.

Time to go and pay Ellie a visit.

28

ELLIE

I've never been one to sleep well after consuming alcohol before bed, which might explain why I am awake and staring at the glowing red digits on my alarm clock. The numbers read **04:17**, and that's not great because I should still be sound asleep now, with it being another three hours or so until my alarm is due to sound. Yet I'm awake, and despite tossing and turning a little bit, I can't drift back off.

I consider visiting the bathroom but worry that will only wake me up further, so I stay where I am, at least warm and cosy under this duvet. I'm not the only one enjoying the comforting blanket because Kyle is beside me, and he is snoring away, deep in slumber and making me feel a little envious that he is re-energising while I am in danger of being extremely tired when I get up for work soon.

Rolling over again, I force my eyes closed and will myself back to sleep before entertaining the idea of counting backwards from 100 in my mind. It will be boring, but that's the idea. However, I'm only on number 91 when I hear a noise outside my bedroom window.

My eyes shoot open, and I look towards the window, but all I see are the closed curtains across it. I definitely heard something, though.

It sounded like something was out there.

Or someone.

I tell myself that it might just be a cat or perhaps a fox roaming around and looking for food. But if it was an animal, why did it sound more like the scraping of a boot, as if a person's foot was passing by right on the other side of the glass?

I listen out intently for any more noises, not expecting to hear it again but fearful in case I do because there is always the chance it might be a burglar. That's the problem with living in a nice property; it attracts interest but not always of the good kind. What if there is a criminal out there now, creeping around, looking for a weakness in the exterior of the house so he can sneak in and try and steal a few things? I don't think we left any windows open, while I'm confident we locked all the doors.

But there's always a chance we missed something.

Thinking about how drunk Kyle and I were when we got home tonight starts to make me paranoid that we have slipped up and left our home vulnerable to an intruder. I didn't put the front door on the latch and assumed Kyle did, but what if he thought I had done it? I was too busy kissing him when we got back to think about that, and what if he got carried away too and forgot all about locking up. However, Kyle's car is on the drive, so I would have thought that suggests somebody is home and would deter any would-be burglar.

Unless they are snooping around to see if they can get the keys for my husband's car.

No, calm down, Ellie. It probably was just an animal; the door is probably locked, and this is probably all in your head.

Nothing to worry about.

You wouldn't have even heard the noise if you were asleep like you should be.

So do that.

Close your eyes.

Go back to sleep.

I'm just about to try and relax again when I hear a noise that has me sitting bolt upright in my bed.

It's the sound of breaking glass, and now I am in no doubts that it isn't an animal out there.

Somebody is breaking in.

By the sounds of it, they have been successful.

'Kyle! Wake up!' I say in an urgent but hushed voice, eager for my husband to hear me but not the person who has apparently just infiltrated our home in the dead of night.

But Kyle isn't easily stirred, clearly in a deep sleep induced by the champagne, which means I have to repeat myself whilst shaking him this time to really increase my chances of bringing him back to consciousness.

As he comes to life, groaning slightly and rolling over to see why I have just disturbed him, I give him the alarming news that nobody who has just been woken up unexpectedly wants to hear.

'I think somebody is in the house!'

My panicked whisper draws the expected reaction from my husband, and Kyle sits upright quickly in bed too, joining me in this fearful state.

'What?'

'I heard a window breaking. Somebody is trying to get in!'

'Are you sure?'

'Yes! I heard a noise outside then I heard glass shattering. I think it might be in the kitchen. They might have come through the back door!'

It's disconcerting to have such a stressful conversation in such whispered tones but not as disconcerting as thinking there is a strange man or woman creeping around on the other side of our closed bedroom door.

'I can't hear anything,' Kyle whispers, and that's annoying because if only he had heard what I had then he would be as worried as me.

'I swear I heard somebody breaking in!' I say, but there's no need for me to try and convince him because a second later, we hear another noise.

Somebody is definitely in here with us.

It might be dark but I see the angst on my husband's face as the reality of this situation dawns on him too, and now we're really in this nightmare together.

'I'll call the police!' I say, reaching for my phone, but just before I can grab it, Kyle stops me.

'No, wait,' he says, though I don't understand why.

'What? We need to call 999. Somebody is in our home, and they might hurt us!' I say, my voice becoming more than a whisper now, and I fear the intruder might just have heard me.

'I'll go and check,' Kyle says, pulling the duvet off and putting his bare feet down onto the carpet.

'No! It's not safe!' I say, pulling him back into the bed, terrified my husband might just be about to walk out of the bedroom and straight into danger.

'It'll be okay,' he says to me, though I have no idea what he is basing that assumption on, so I plead with him again to just let me call the police and have them come to investigate. With a bit of luck, the intruder will either be caught or leave without entering the bedroom, and as long as we are okay, I don't care if he makes off with a few of our possessions along the way. But Kyle seems eager for me to not get the police involved, which I don't understand, and he pulls away from me and approaches the door.

'Kyle!' I whisper to him, getting out of bed myself, and while he tells me to stay where I am, I don't listen to him, joining him by the door, shielding myself behind him but eager to stay close because I want to try and protect him too.

Kyle takes hold of the door handle and gently turns it, and I almost feel like I can hear his heartbeat, as well as mine, as the door opens, and we peer out into the dark hallway beyond our bedroom. But before I can follow him out, he tells me to stay here.

'No, I want to stay with you,' I say, but he shakes his head and urges me to stay.

I guess it's his protective nature taking over as the man of the house, but he clearly wants to go by himself, so I do what he tells me and stay where I am.

Watching Kyle creeping away down the hallway is unnerving, and it's just as tense when he calls out to whoever might be in the house that the police have been called and they better leave before they get into any trouble. But there is no response to that.

The intruder is quiet.

Too quiet.

Kyle tries again, saying he knows that somebody is in here and they have ten seconds to get out or they'll regret it, but again, there is no word from any burglar.

Have they already left?

Or are they lurking in the shadows, waiting to pounce?

'Kyle,' I whisper to my husband, but he doesn't answer, too focused on going forward rather than back again, and as I watch him disappear around the corner to where the staircase is, I lose sight of him and feel even more frantic.

'Kyle?' I whisper, but there is no answer, and I'm not sure what to do when I suddenly hear him cry out in what sounds like pain.

'KYLE!' I shout as I run from the bedroom, showing no fear of entering danger myself because I just want to make sure my husband is okay. But as I round the corner and look down the stairs, I get my answer, and it's not the answer I was hoping for.

'Kyle! No!' I cry when I see the man I love lying on the steps below me clutching his abdomen, his t-shirt soaked in blood and his eyes already closed.

Then I see the person who has stabbed him.

They are standing over his body, a knife in one hand and a wicked grin on their face.

It's not just any intruder.

I recognise this man.

And he knows me too.

'Hello, Ellie,' Harvey says as the bloodied knife glints in the moonlight from the hallway window. 'It's been a while, hasn't it?'

29

DAWN

The frantic phone call I made to the police as I drove to Ellie's place seems to have done the trick because no sooner have I arrived on the street then I see blue flashing lights coming to join me.

Having dialled 999 and told the operator that my daughter had fallen victim to a pair of criminals who were not only capable of scamming her but keeping me imprisoned, I implored them to send police cars to Kyle's address. I assumed I would get there first but underestimated the response time of the local police force, and as I get out of my car, I see three other police cars parking nearby.

No doubt the fact I told the operator that I thought my daughter's life might be in danger helped expedite their response, but I'm glad they're here now because maybe I was right and Ellie could be hurt by Kyle, not just financially but physically too.

'This is the house,' I say, pointing to the front door as I run up the driveway, and while the first police officer to reach me asks me to slow down, I do no such thing.

'Go in there and arrest Kyle!' I say. 'Do it now before things get any worse.'

I am about to try the front door myself when another police officer tells me they will take it from here, and I am pulled to the side before two more officers knock on the door to establish if anybody is in. But this is all happening too slowly for me.

'Just kick the door down!' I cry. 'That man in there with my daughter is dangerous!'

As I make my emphatic statement, I'm wondering if any of these officers recognise me from the last time I was embroiled in a drama in this town. If so, they might think I'm just having some form of flashback to that time and massively overexaggerating, or even imagining, what is going on. But they have a duty to check out any reports of a crime, which is what they are doing, although surely not quickly enough.

As I see two officers go around the back of the house, I am just wishing somebody would hurry up and go inside, but a moment later, I hear chatter over the radios that there are signs of forced entry at the rear.

Forced entry?

That seems to be the cue for the police at the front door to go inside, and they enter with force of their own, kicking the door in and loudly announcing their arrival in the hallway.

As I'm ordered to wait outside with an officer keeping me company, I'm praying that I will see Ellie emerge in a moment in her pyjamas, confused and demanding to know what is going on, though I will quickly explain to her once she does. I'm also praying that I will see Kyle come out in handcuffs and be marched right past me on the way to the backseat of a police car. When that happens, I will gladly hurl a few insults his way so he is left in no doubt as to how I feel about him and his rotten partner, who will shortly be in police custody too.

But nobody comes out of the house, and all I hear are the radios belonging to the police officers around me come to life, and suddenly, it's as if the urgency amongst them kicks into a higher gear. Two more officers rush into the house while I hear another officer radioing for further help. That's when I start to panic that we're too late.

Has Kyle already hurt Ellie and made off with the money she took out for him?

Has he gone?

And is she dead?

'What is it? What's happening?' I cry, and I try to go to the front door, but I'm held back and told that it is an active crime scene, and I'm not allowed inside.

'My daughter is in there! Is she okay?' I beg to know, but I don't get any answer, and that is telling.

Oh my God. Something horrible has happened to Ellie. She has come to harm again, and unlike last time, I haven't been able to save her when she needed me.

My legs are losing all their power, and I feel like I could collapse on this driveway and cry for days but just before I do, a police officer emerges from the house, and he has an update for me.

'There is no sign of any female in the property,' I'm told.

'What? Where's my daughter?' I ask, but the officer doesn't seem to know. However, he doesn't seem to be relaxing either, which tells me that while he didn't find Ellie in there, he has found something.

'Where's Kyle?' I ask. 'My daughter's husband! Or fake husband, whatever he is! Is he inside?'

The officer shares a concerned look with a colleague before I'm told that I will have to step back and allow the police to do their work here.

'What's going on?' I beg to know, but I'm still no nearer to having any clue, though things quickly get busier on the street.

At first, I see all the neighbours turning on their lights, and a few of them open their front doors and come outside in their dressing gowns, clearly keen to find out what all the commotion is about.

But it's not the addition of the neighbours that makes this whole scene more difficult.

It's the addition of the ambulance, along with a big, white van, from which emerges several forensic experts in white overalls.

'Please tell me what is happening!' I beg with tears running down my cheeks as I see paramedics enter the house, and even though I was told that there were no females inside the property, clearly something awful has happened here, and with the forensic team on site too, I'm guessing it involves a death.

Maybe it is Ellie whose body they have found, and they just don't want to break the news to me yet because I'll make things more difficult for them to get on with the job at hand. An officer might ask me to come to the station shortly, and that might be where they are finally honest with me and admit that they did find Ellie in the house and, sadly, there was nothing they could do for her.

But if it is bad news of the very worst kind, it doesn't matter where I hear it because it will ruin my life whether I'm standing on a cold street or sitting in a meeting room at the station. That's why I keep urging anybody who will listen to me to just tell me what is going on, though over an hour goes by without me getting any answers, and I can see the sun starting to crest on the horizon over the tops of all these houses.

Finally, after the sky has turned from a dark black to a pale blue, I get somebody competent enough, or simply qualified enough, to give me an answer.

'Upon entering the property, the officers discovered the body of a male on the staircase,' comes the grim report. 'He was the only person inside the house, so, as of yet, we don't know where your daughter is.'

The body of a male?

'Is it Kyle?' I ask, confused as to how he could have ended up being the victim here when I thought that was Ellie.

'We believe so,' I'm told before I'm asked if I know where else my daughter might be.

'No, but you need to find her because she might be hurt too!' I try, although, to my surprise, the officer doesn't seem to be thinking along the same lines as me.

'Is it possible that your daughter could have harmed her partner?' comes the next question.

'Excuse me?'

'You told us that your daughter was being tricked by a man she believed to be her husband. Is it possible she might have found out about that and retaliated?'

'You think Ellie hurt Kyle? No, she wouldn't do that,' I say, and at that exact moment, our heated conversation is halted by the appearance of a body bag being removed from the house.

I stare at the white bag as it is carried past me and loaded into the back of the van, and as the doors close behind it, I see several of the neighbours out here putting their hands to their mouths to cover their shock.

They are disbelieving.

They are confused.

But they are only feeling a fraction of what I am as I try to make sense of what has happened.

Kyle is dead, but how did it happen? I heard there were signs of forced entry, so does that mean an intruder put him in that body bag? Or, as the police officer who I was just speaking to seemed to suggest, could it have been my daughter who hurt him?

I'd like to think not, or at least she wouldn't have hurt him unless her own life was in danger. But if it had been, surely she would have just called the police and reported what had happened. Yet she seems to be missing now, and an innocent person doesn't leave the scene of a crime, do they? They stay and explain what happened because they want to help.

Yet Ellie is nowhere to be seen.

Is my daughter innocent? Or did she do what I felt like doing when I was tied up back at Julia's flat? Did she kill Kyle once she realised what a scumbag he was?

I don't know.

The police, nor any of these neighbours, don't seem to know either.

The only person who will know is Ellie herself.

But where is she?

30

ELLIE

It's only been ten minutes since I saw Kyle's body on the staircase and realised my husband was dead but, in that time, I feel as if I've already expunged every tear that my body is capable of producing.

I dropped to my knees and wept as I tried to bring Kyle back to life, and I kept crying even when it was clear there was no saving him. I continued to cry as Harvey grabbed a hold of me and dragged me down the stairs, and I struggled to answer him through my tears when he told me that I had to cooperate with him or else.

I kept crying all through the part where he told me that I was going to pay for what had happened to his son, and I was still sobbing when he started to demand that I give him the keys to Kyle's car so he could drive us both away. After Harvey threatened to stab me with the same knife he had murdered Kyle with, I was forced into telling him where the car keys were, and then I was dragged to the door, crying as I went because even though he was already gone, I didn't want to leave the body of my poor partner behind.

But it was as I was pushed into the passenger seat of the car that my tears ceased, and as Harvey turned on the engine and reversed us off the driveway, I simply started to feel very cold. I assumed I was going into shock; that would be the only explanation for the calming chill that came over me, and it must have been my brain's way of figuring out how to get me through the next several minutes.

It was almost as if I was blocking out what had just happened because it was too much for me to process all at once, and it would need to be dealt with at a later date. That's when I went quiet and still, and I have been that way since as Harvey has driven us on, and I quickly realised we were headed in the direction of Mum's house.

'What have you done to her?' I ask the deadly American man I'm sitting beside, terrified of the answer because it might be that she has already suffered the same fate as Kyle and I've lost two people I care about tonight instead of just one.

'It's good to see you again, Ellie,' Harvey replies, ignoring my question as he steers us around a corner. 'You have no idea how much time I spent in prison visualising your face and your mother's and patiently waiting until I could surprise you like this.'

'Where is my mum?' I cry, but Harvey simply replies with the cold callousness that he clearly passed down to his son on the night he tried to kill me in the park near here.

'Do what I say, and you will see your mum again,' he tells me. 'But resist and it will not end well for you.'

That's my clear warning not to try and fight back, force the car off the road and try and open my door and run. But I couldn't run even if I wanted to, not just because I am worried about Mum and want to see if she is okay but because I feel too weak to even mount an escape considering the trauma I have just suffered.

My husband is dead. My husband, who I only married a few days ago. We were supposed to be together for the rest of our lives. Happy ever after.

But now I'm a widow.

Just like Mum.

I think about how she hasn't sent me a message or called me all day, and now I can see why. Harvey must have gone to her first and silenced her. Is she tied up at home? In pain? Clinging on to life or already gone? I don't know, and I'm not going to know until we get to her house.

My state of shock continues to keep me functioning somewhat for as long as it takes Harvey to park outside Mum's place, but I start to struggle again when he tells me to get out of the car.

'No,' I say because now that we're here, I feel like this is Harvey's final way to torment me. He's going to take me into Mum's house and show me her dead body, and then, when I'm totally devastated, he will kill me, and this will all be over. If that's his plan, I'd rather he just killed me here.

'I can't,' I say after Harvey has repeated his instruction for me to get out of the car.

'Yes, you can!' he cries, clearly frustrated, and he runs around to my door before opening it and dragging me out. Then he pushes me towards the back of the house, though as we go, I see something that gives me hope that Mum might not be in here and hurt or dead.

Her car isn't on the driveway.

If Harvey had come here first and harmed her, surely he would have driven to me in her vehicle. But he needed the keys to Kyle's car to get us here, so maybe he hasn't found Mum yet.

If so, maybe I can try and escape.

I turn and attempt to run, terrified that I'll feel a knife penetrating my skin if I fail in getting away quickly. But while I don't feel a blade going into me, I do feel Harvey's strong hand grab one of my arms, and I'm pulled back towards him before I'm dragged around the side of the house and into the back garden. I see Harvey take out a key then, and he opens the back door with it, which tells me he must have already been here and accessed the property earlier, though the sight of a broken window nearby could also tell me that too.

'What are you doing?' I ask Harvey once I'm inside, and he has told me to sit down on one of the kitchen chairs, but he ignores me as he re-locks the back door before starting to check some of the cupboards in here, clearly looking for something, though I'm not sure what.

'Where is my mum? Her car isn't on the drive. She's not here, is she? Where is she?'

My questions continue to frustrate my captor, but after he has failed to answer, I ask him about the man he just killed.

'Why did you hurt my husband? He didn't know you. He didn't know Daryl either. If this is about me and Mum, why did you have to kill him?'

'Shut up!' Harvey cries, and he's clearly getting fed up with me, which may be a good thing or a bad thing. It might be promising that he's looking a little flustered because it might be that he isn't as in control of this situation as I first thought he was. But it might be a bad thing if he decides that he could simply get me to be quiet by plunging the knife into my stomach.

So maybe I had better follow his order.

Saying nothing, I continue to watch him before he tells me to stay where I am if I want to see my mum again. Then he leaves the room for a moment, going through the door that leads into the garage, and once I'm alone, I wonder if I could try and make another run for it.

I saw Harvey lock the back door, but I could try and break through it, or maybe I could run to the front door and try that. Whatever I decide, I have to try something, so I get up and run through out of the kitchen, praying that somehow, the front door was left unlocked by Mum. But it won't open, and a second later, Harvey has his hands on me again, dragging me back into the kitchen where he reminds me that if I don't do as he says, I will die.

I have no choice but to sit back down on the chair after he has brandished the knife at me, but I also see something else he has. *Ropes.* They must be what he was looking for, and now he has located them in the garage, he is using them to tie me to this chair.

Once I'm restrained, Harvey finally relaxes, and after putting the back door key in the lock, presumably so he won't lose it if he needs to leave here quickly, he takes a seat opposite me.

'We're going to wait here until your mum gets home,' he says. 'Do you know where she is?'

She's okay. He hasn't hurt her yet.

'No, I don't, but you aren't going to get away with this, you scumbag!' I cry. 'She's too smart for you, just like she was too smart for your son. That's why he's dead, and you're going to die too!'

It might not be the wisest thing I've ever said, but I had to get it off my chest, and boy, did it feel good. But annoyingly, Harvey doesn't react to my outburst, probably because, for now, he retains the upper hand in this situation.

But for how long?

31

DAWN

Since I was brought to the police station after all the drama at Kyle and Ellie's house, I have been asked a few things. I was asked if I wanted a hot drink. I was asked if I had any idea what might have happened at the crime scene we had just been at. And most of all, I have been asked if I have any idea where my daughter might be.

But my answer to all those questions has been the same.

No.

However, while the answer to the question about the drink was met with indifference, my answers to the other two questions have not been. The police are desperate to know what happened at that house and how Kyle came to be stabbed to death on his staircase, but I am no different to them.

I want to know what the hell happened as well.

I also want to make it clear that neither I or my daughter had anything to do with it.

'Ellie wouldn't have stabbed him,' I say, shaking my head at the female detective sitting opposite me. 'She loved him. He was her husband. They only recently got married.'

'But you have told us that Kyle was a con man who tricked her into taking out a large bank loan that he planned to run away with,' the detective calmly replies.

'Yes, but Ellie didn't know that!' I cry. 'I was on my way to tell her. She had no idea she was being lied to! I only found out yesterday!'

'So you say,' the detective replies, checking her notes. 'You said you followed Kyle to a flat and saw him with another woman before you approached her, and she attacked you and imprisoned you for several hours before you were able to escape.'

'That's right. You know it happened. I told you where to go to find the flat and the woman inside. Julia! She had me tied up, but I got away. If I hadn't then who knows what might have happened to me!'

'Our officers have gone to that flat, and we have found Julia,' the detective tells me. 'She was tied up.'

'Yes, I know! Because I tied her up, but only because she did the same thing to me earlier!'

'There was also a lot of her blood on the floor of the flat.'

'She ran across broken glass,' I say before the detective can think that I was the one who drew that blood from Julia myself. 'She's the one who attacked me. I just got away!'

'It's funny because Julia has told us that you are the one who attacked her,' comes the shocking reply.

'What?'

'You see, we're getting differing stories here, so right now, I don't know what to believe.'

'You have to believe me because I'm the one telling the truth! Julia and Kyle were working as a team to trick my daughter into getting them a lot of money, and from what Julia told me, the plan had almost worked. Check with the bank. See how big of a loan my daughter took out yesterday. It'll be £100,000. She got that money for Kyle because she thought his business was in trouble, but he planned to run away with it and leave my daughter with the debt. They are criminals, and they've done this to other people before. Ellie wasn't the first!'

'Wow, that's quite a tale,' the detective says, looking almost impressed by the story I have just come up with.

'It's the truth,' I say, exasperated. 'I swear I'm telling you the truth. Where is Julia now? Are you questioning her?'

'Yes, we are, and we will get to the bottom of what is going on here.'

'Good, but you have to be quicker because my daughter is missing, and whoever killed Kyle must have her somewhere now. You saw signs of forced entry at the house, right? Whoever broke in must have stabbed Kyle and then taken Ellie somewhere.'

'Who would do such a thing like that?'

'I don't know. Maybe somebody who Kyle scammed before. They might have found him and come for revenge.'

It's clear that's not what the detective wanted to hear, or perhaps it only confirms what she suspects, which is that this isn't some crazy plot that needs unravelling but a very simple case of a vengeful wife killing her lying husband.

'Ellie's not a murderer,' I say under my breath, completely convinced that my child is incapable of harming another human being.

'But you are,' the detective replies.

Oh no. Here we go again. My past is about to rear its ugly head one more time.

'I understand you and your daughter were involved in an incident just over five years ago in which a young man lost his life,' the detective tells me, not looking at her notes anymore because she obviously knows all about what happened before.

'A young man who was trying to kill my daughter,' I tell her, also not needing notes because I see visions of that dark park in my dreams every night, as well as Daryl's lifeless body lying by my feet and a bloodied rock in my hand. 'What's your point?'

'My point is, you and your family are no stranger to dead bodies and police investigations. Has your daughter followed your lead and killed now, or has history repeated itself and you were the one who ended Kyle's life? Should we be looking at you as a suspect?'

'This is ridiculous!'

'Is it? You really expect me to believe it's just one big coincidence that a normal suburban mother and daughter have ended up at the centre of two of the biggest crimes that have ever happened in this town?'

'Yes!'

'So you believe in coincidences?'

'Yes. I mean, no. I mean, I'm not sure.'

'I don't believe in them. Do you know what I believe in? Patterns. History. Habits. The past playing out in the present. Those are far greater indicators of what has really happened rather than some whimsical thought about a bit of bad luck and misfortune and two people like you and your daughter just being in the wrong place at the wrong time again.'

I think about defending myself one more time, but it seems pointless. I also think about what the detective has just said, and despite it not helping me, I know she is mostly right. The past is often a far better predictor of the future than anything.

The past…

Daryl…

Harvey.

'Oh my God,' I say as I get up from my chair, surprising the detective with my sudden movement. 'What if this has nothing to do with Kyle and Julia? What if this is linked to what happened before?'

'What are you talking about?'

'What if Daryl's dad has come back to get revenge, and now he has Ellie!'

It takes me a few minutes to make the detective understand what I am saying, but after I tell her about how Harvey recently got out of prison and then immediately travelled to Europe, I suggest he might have found his way into England and tracked my daughter down.

'He could have broken into that house and killed Kyle when confronted by him!' I cry. 'And then he's taken Ellie away. That explains why we can't find her!'

'But if he has her, where would they be?'

I have to think about that one but not for long because if Harvey has come for Ellie, there's no way he wouldn't want to pay me a visit too. I was the one who dealt his son's fatal blow, after all.

'My house,' I say. 'They'd be at my house.'

'Hang on a minute, I can't just entertain these wild theories when there is a serious crime to be investigating,' the detective says, but I tell her again how certain I am that I am right. I also give her a reason to give me a chance.

'If I'm wrong about this then do whatever you want. Arrest me. Charge me for Kyle's death. Throw away the key; I don't care. But if I'm right then we have to go to my house now because my daughter will be there, and she will be in danger!'

It might have been down to my impassioned pleas or simply because the detective was lacking better options at the time, but she agreed to go along with my plan, and two minutes later, I am in a police car that is racing towards my house, along with several other cars, one of which holds the detective.

It all comes down to this.

Am I wrong?

Or is Harvey here?

If he is, maybe it's his turn to give me an unhappy ending.

32

ELLIE

It's strange to be feeling so afraid and helpless in the house I grew up in.

This is my family home.

I should be secure here. Strong here. Feel safer here than anywhere else in the world.

It's the place I used to play as a child, where I would have bedtime stories read to me and watch cartoons and run around making too much noise simply because I was young and excited. It's also the place I sat with my parents and had meals, listened to them talk about their day, their plans for the weekend, how tired work made them feel, how it was only a few weeks to go until we all went on holiday again. I have hugged my mum and dad in every room of this house, and inside this building, there is a lot of love and warmth that will never dissipate, no matter how much time passes.

Sure, there have been bad times too, like when I would cry after falling over and hurting myself or refuse to eat some vegetable and be told that I had to stay at the table until it was gone. The long nights of revising for exams when I felt like I wasn't clever enough or the times I would lie on my bed and wait for a boy I liked to text me back, only to go to sleep upset and lonely when he didn't. Then of course, there were the worst times, the time when Dad was ill and I could see him getting weaker, no longer able to do the things he used to be able to do. The time when Mum and I came home after the funeral and realised it was just the two of us now instead of three. And all the times we argued, not because we hated each other but because we were both so upset that we were simply trying to make the other one feel worse so we might feel a little better. But even through all those bad times, this was still my home. I still always felt safe here, never scared. I might have grown bored of these four walls at times or wished to be somewhere else, but I always knew that of all the places in the world, this was where I belonged the most, whether I liked it at the time or not.

Yet tonight, as I sit here tied to this chair and look at the man with the knife in his hand, I finally feel it.

This home is no longer a safe place for me or my mum.

This house is dangerous now.

'Looks like it's going to be a nice day,' Harvey says as he nods towards the sunlight streaming through the broken kitchen window, though I don't turn and look because the weather can't help me here. 'I thought it just rained all the time in England, but I guess not.'

Harvey leans back a little further in his seat, causing the chair to creak, and as I hear the noise, it gives me a flashback to when Dad would sit at this table with me and fill the chair in the same way. I wish he was here now. He'd protect me. He'd get rid of this man. He would never allow me or Mum to be threatened in our own home.

'Your mother really does work long hours, doesn't she?' Harvey says, almost with a respectful tone.

'It's funny because I bet she can't wait to get home, but really, the longer she stays away from here, the safer she is.'

He checks his watch then before letting out a sigh, and it's clear that while he is trying to look calm, he is impatient to get on with this. But, seemingly, he refuses to do anything more until Mum is here to witness it.

'What's your plan?' I ask him. You're going to kill me in front of Mum? Then what? Kill her? Walk out the door and go back to LA? Get away with it? You really think it's going to be that simple?'

'I didn't say anything about going back to LA or getting away with it,' Harvey replies, and that answer chills my bones.

'So you're happy to go to prison for the rest of your life? Didn't you just get out of there? I guess it's not as bad as people say it is if you're happy to go straight back.'

'Oh, it is bad,' Harvey tells me with a look on his face that makes it obvious he saw some grim things during his time inside. 'But I'd rather be in there and know I did everything for my son than be out here and feel like I failed him.'

'But you did fail him,' I say, and Harvey wasn't expecting that answer. 'You weren't there to help him that night he died, and nothing you can do now will ever change that fact. All you are doing here is making your own miserable life worse.'

'Shut up!' Harvey cries, getting up from his seat and taking the knife with him, but I carry on goading him to see if I can at least get him to do something other than wait for Mum to come back.

'Your son needed his father when he died, and you weren't there,' I go on. 'Now he's in hell, but it's okay because you'll be joining him soon. You'll be right there with him because - guess what? Mum is a better parent than you, and she won't let me come to harm like Daryl did. She'll fight for me, and she'll save me, and I'll survive while Daryl will still be dead!'

I instantly regret my taunts when Harvey rushes towards me, and he only stops when the blade is an inch from my throat.

'Say one more word,' he dares me. 'Say one more word about my son and see what happens.'

That's the moment when I realise I would be better off shutting up or I won't live to see Mum come home and try and save me, so I do as I'm told and keep quiet.

'I thought so,' Harvey says before he moves the knife away from my throat and goes back to his seat. But just before he can retake it, we hear the sound of a car outside, and when we hear doors opening and closing too, we both think the same thing.

'Sounds like somebody is home,' Harvey says with a smile, and he rushes to the front of the house to take a look. But no sooner has he disappeared then he comes running back into the room again and double-checks the lock on the back door, trying the handle and ensuring it can't be opened.

'What are you doing?' I ask him, but Harvey looks distracted, almost like he didn't even hear me.

'Harvey?' I try again, and this time, he hears me.

'The police are here,' he says, and in that second, I don't think I've ever heard a better sentence in my whole life.

'It's over!' I say. 'Run now or they'll catch you,' I cry, praying that he will just leave but aware that him making sure the door was locked is more an indicator that he is bunkering down rather than looking to evacuate.

'How?' Harvey says under his breath before he takes a deep breath and approaches me again.

'I guess I'll just have to adapt,' he says, and while I'm not sure what he means by that, I feel the cold edge of the blade on my throat again as he stands behind me and tells me to stay quiet whilst he unties me. But if I think he's letting me go, I am wrong because as he pulls me to my feet, he keeps the knife over my windpipe.

We both hear a key turning in the front door, and a moment later, I hear Mum's voice filling the house.

'Ellie? Are you here?'

'Mum!' I cry instinctively, but no sooner have I made my own noise then the blade presses further into my throat, and Harvey whispers in my ear that he will cut me open if I don't shut up.

'Ellie?' Mum calls out again, presumably having heard me, but I'm not in a position to be able to say anything more, though I don't need to when we're joined in the kitchen by Mum and two police officers.

They freeze instantly when they see the hostage scenario they have just walked into, and Harvey quickly lays out the facts for them so there can be no confusion.

'Come any closer and I'll cut her throat,' he says, his voice haunting and loud as it comes so close to my right ear. 'You hear me? Stay back!'

Mum and the officers do as they are told and remain by the doorway before Harvey gives them another instruction.

'Dawn stays here. Everybody else out!'

'Harvey, just calm down. Everything's going to be okay,' Mum tries, but Harvey only grips me tighter and makes it clear he isn't in the mood for discussing this.

'Everybody out!' he says before he briefly moves the knife away from my throat and points the end of it at Mum. 'Except you.'

The police officers are obviously reluctant to leave two civilians in such a perilous position, but Mum tells them to go, and very quickly, they also receive instruction from another person who enters the room, a woman in a suit who must be in charge of them. As they go, the one in the suit tells Harvey that they will communicate with him shortly, but in the meantime, they request he doesn't do anything stupid. But Harvey holds all the power in this situation, the police well aware that one false move and they will be responsible for him killing me, so they eventually do as he asked of them and leave.

Now it's just me, him and Mum in this house.

We're surrounded on the outside.

But Harvey doesn't seem too bothered about that.

Maybe because he knows none of us are getting out of here alive.

33

DAWN

Is this the most frightening scenario a parent could ever find themselves in?

I'm currently watching my daughter being held at knifepoint in my own home, and there is nothing I can do about it. Not only that but she isn't being held by just anybody. This might not be so bad if it was some intruder who simply wanted to know where I kept my valuables. That would be fine because I'd happily give them up to keep Ellie safe. But this is worse because this isn't about money.

It's about revenge.

So that probably means this will only end one way.

I've already tried getting Harvey to lower the knife, but he has so far refused, insisting that I keep my distance from him and Ellie, and I have had to do that, only the kitchen table standing between me and my daughter. I want nothing more than to run to her and pull her away from this dangerous man and then hold her tightly and tell her that everything will be okay as the police swoop in. But I might not be able to do that, and failing my daughter when she is alive frightens me just as much as having to deal with her dead body, if this all goes as Harvey clearly wants it to.

'You're surrounded. You have nowhere to go,' I remind Harvey. 'You saw the police. They're here. They're everywhere. You'll never get out of this now, so just put the knife down and don't make things any worse for yourself.'

'Don't make things any worse for myself? They can't get any worse! I just spent the last five years in prison, and my son is dead! You think I give a damn about the police?'

That's a very scary answer because it tells me Harvey has nothing to lose and might not care about getting out of here alive. But I care about that, as does my daughter, and the tears running down her cheeks are proof.

'It's going to be okay, darling,' I say, trying to calm her, but Harvey just scoffs at that.

'It's not nice, is it?' he asks me. 'To know your child is in danger and there is nothing you can do about it. That's what I felt like when my son died here, by your hand, and I was in America, helpless.'

'You know why I had to do it,' I plead. 'He was going to hurt Ellie! I never would have hurt him if he hadn't been violent himself!'

Harvey shakes his head, clearly not going to entertain anything I can say regarding my reasons for killing Daryl, though as he does, I notice movement through the broken window behind him. Police officers are creeping around out there, clearly ensuring all exits are covered, though at the moment, that isn't helping the problem inside the house, and when Harvey spots them, he shouts at them to stay away, which they do, retreating out of view.

'He killed Kyle,' Ellie says, terrible pain in her voice, and as she does, I remember that, as of this moment, she has no idea who Kyle really was and the lies he told her. Should I tell her now? Would that help ease some of her pain? Or would it make her feel even worse if she finds out in such a high-pressure situation like this?

Maybe I should leave that until later.

If there is a later.

'Harvey, please. Just let Ellie go. I'm the one you want. I killed your son,' I say, sacrificing myself for my daughter, but that's okay because rather me than her. But Ellie doesn't like that idea and wants both of us to be let go. But what does Harvey want?

'You wish to lay down your life to save your child,' he says, the blade over Ellie's throat glinting for a second when it catches a ray of early morning sunlight filtering through the window behind him. 'What a brave thing to do, yet what an obvious thing to do too. Any parent would make that sacrifice. I would have made that sacrifice. Except I never had the chance, and now it's too late.'

'Harvey, please-'

'No, Dawn. It's time for you to shut up and listen to me,' Harvey goes on. 'It's time for you to know the pain I feel. The pain of losing the person you love most in the world. That powerless feeling. I want you to have that feeling too, because you deserve it. You took my boy from me, and I don't care what the circumstances were. You removed the life from him, and now it's time for me to get my own back.'

I see the blade start to move, and Ellie cries out, so I rush forward and try to grab hold of Harvey's arm before he can make the damage irreparable. But he suddenly jabs the knife out towards me, and I am only just able to stop my momentum before I become impaled on it myself.

'Stay back!' Harvey cries as I see more police officers through the window, but so far, none of them have been any help to me.

As Harvey begins to circle away from the window and towards the back door, I fear he will see the police officers again too, though they quickly move when they realise the suspect is moving himself.

As Harvey slowly walks around the kitchen table with Ellie still in his grasp, I start to slowly circle too, following his rules and keeping my distance. But as I move, I pass the fridge and see the photo of Sean, and just a quick glimpse of his image gives me the inner strength to not give up here.

'What good will hurting Ellie do?' I ask Harvey. 'It won't bring Daryl back. It'll just make things worse.'

'For you,' he replies, still slowly moving around the table, and as he does, he looks outside the window, spotting a couple of officers and seemingly becoming even more distressed at their presence.

'No, for everybody,' I say. 'Why don't you just put the knife down and let Ellie go? If you want me to stay here with you then that's fine. I'll stay, and you can say whatever it is you want to say to me. You can use the knife if you want to. Maybe both of us will not leave this kitchen alive. But let Ellie go. Come on, Harvey, you know she's innocent, and she's already lost her husband. She'll be in pain forever for that, trust me, I know. She's had enough. Let her go. Let's just make this about you and me. It's not about our kids anymore, is it? It's about me and you.'

Harvey seems to be listening to what I am saying and accepts that it is about me and him, though he still hasn't removed the knife from in front of Ellie's throat yet. But as he nears the fridge, he momentarily looks at the photo of me with my late husband. As he does that, I reach the back door and see the key is in the lock. I also see the silhouettes of several police officers on the other side of the frosted glass.

They're eager to get in.

Maybe I can make it easier for them.

'Look at that photo,' I say to Harvey, keen for him to keep his eyes on the fridge and not on me as I reach the door with my back to it. 'Look at that man smiling beside me and Ellie in the photo and realise that I have already lost someone I care about. I don't need to lose anybody else. You want me to know what pain is? Well, I know. Trust me, I do.'

Harvey is still looking at the photo as he slowly shuffles around and as he does, I reach out and quickly turn the key, unlocking the door, though it remains closed for now. Harvey hasn't noticed my sneaky move, but as he moves past the fridge, leading Ellie with him, he returns his gaze to me.

'You can say whatever you want,' he tells me. 'But I didn't come all this way to not finish what I started, or finish what my son started, for that matter. He wanted Ellie dead. That was his choice to make. He didn't get to kill her, but I will and then, when I'm done,

I'll have mercy on you, Dawn, and kill you too. Your pain will end then. How does that sound?'

I stay where I am by the back door, but Harvey tells me to move, using the knife to point the way, and I start walking around the kitchen table then, giving him some space. But as he gets closer to the back door, he has no idea that it is unlocked now, and there is very little between him and the focused officers outside.

Harvey stops pacing, holding Ellie as tightly as ever, and then looks me dead in the eyes. Then he says this is over, and I'm sure he expects me to beg for one more chance before he kills my daughter.

But I don't do that.

All I do is agree with him.

'You're right,' I say, confidently and clearly. 'It is over. But only for you.'

Harvey is confused by that statement, but he figures out what I mean a second later when I let out a deafening cry.

'The back door is unlocked! Get him!'

The door suddenly flies open, and as Harvey turns in horror, he is quickly tackled by a burly officer who forces the knife from his hand as Ellie runs away from him and towards me.

As I pull my daughter in and refuse to let go, I watch as Harvey is handcuffed on my kitchen floor before he is pulled to his feet and dragged out of my house, heading back to a place he is already familiar with.

A prison cell.

Thankfully, I won't have to go back to a place I'm familiar with now this is over. Ellie has survived, meaning I won't have another reason to visit the local graveyard. My husband's headstone is more than enough.

My daughter is safe.

I have saved her again.

As we hug, I catch a glimpse of Sean's smiling face on the fridge photo beside us.

34

ELLIE

I remember when I was younger and my dad would often joke about what he would do when I got to the age when boyfriends were turning up at my door to take me out.

He said he would be rigorously vetting all of them, ensuring they were suitable candidates to be dating his offspring and keeping an eye on them and me to make sure nothing bad might happen. The overprotective dad routine is surely something that goes on in every household between a father and daughter, and while I would secretly dread the idea of Dad making life difficult for any of my partners, I knew he only wanted the best for me and would welcome in any guy who treated me with as much care as he did himself.

I also knew he would make life hell for any man who treated me badly.

With that in mind, it might not have been a terrible thing that he hasn't been around to see some of my past partners because I would have definitely caused him enough stress. As it is, Mum has had to shoulder all that stress, and she has somehow managed it.

But what about me?

How unlucky in love can one girl be?

It's weird, but as time has gone on since the drama with Harvey, I feel like things could have been worse. Losing Kyle seemed like the worst thing in the world at the time, but that's only because I thought he was my loving husband. However, once the dust had settled and Mum had told me who he really was and that we weren't even actually married, I didn't feel quite as bad as I would have if I had genuinely become a heartbroken widow. It's not quite the same when instead of finding out the man who died was the love of your life, they're actually nothing more than a common criminal who lived for telling lies and didn't have an ounce of compassion for me at all.

I was stung by the truth that Kyle had simply targeted me and tricked me into falling in love with him before going one step further and tricking me into taking out a huge bank loan that he planned to disappear with. I was also hurt when I found out about his accomplice, Julia, his real love, and how the pair of them routinely conspired to deceive innocent people like me all the time. Meanwhile, the police were a little happier when they learned of the pair of scam artists because they had been after them for a while, seeking out the tricksters who had scammed other people out of fortunes for the last several years.

While Kyle was dead, Julia was still alive to be punished, and punished she will be as she currently resides in a jail cell awaiting trial for numerous offences. There is a long line of witnesses waiting for their chance to testify against her, and Mum and I will be right there in the witness box when the time comes for us to have our say.

I can't wait.

Regarding the bank loan I took out, because not a penny of it had been spent before Kyle and Julia's plan was exposed and because it turned out I was the victim of a crime, there have been no consequences there. The money was simply returned to the bank, meaning I have incurred no debt, which is not something I would have been able to say if Kyle and Julia's plan had been successful. As well as that, the bank actually apologised to me and admitted they should have conducted more stringent checks when I requested the loan, realising that I could have been a victim instead of just taking my word for it that I simply needed £100,000 as if it was a simple transaction customers make every single day. In a bid to show they were sorry, or most likely simply because they wanted to put a positive spin on all the bad press they had been getting about how they had so easily given up so much money that was to be used for criminal gains, the bank offered me a goodwill gesture to bring the whole sorry matter to a close.

I got £5,000 from them in exchange for making sure I made it public and went on record with a journalist to say how good the bank was with its customers and how this type of thing didn't usually happen, which went a long way to restoring the trust in the compromised financial institution.

What will I spend that money on? Let's just say I have an idea, or rather it was Mum's idea, but what exactly that is will remain between me and her.

So, how is Mum doing after I helped put her through yet more drama? She's actually doing rather well, as evidenced by the fact that she is currently getting ready to go on a date.

I'm lying on the sofa in my childhood home, scoffing crisps and watching television but breaking off occasionally from my lazy fun to judge the various outfits Mum is showing to me every time she walks into the room.

'What do you think of this one?' she asks me as she gives me a twirl, and I regard the flowery, blue dress with admiration before telling her I think we've found the one.

That's a relief because Mum's spent the last hour changing into various dresses and parading around in them to get my critical opinion, but finally, it seems progress has been made and not a moment too late because her date is due to begin within the hour.

'Right, I better go and put my make-up on. I don't want to scare away my date in the first few seconds,' Mum says, her self-deprecating humour making me smile as she leaves the room, and I go back to eating my snacks.

Do I feel bad that Mum is the one going out for a fun evening with a handsome guy while I'm the one stuck at home with nowhere to go and no one to be wined and dined by?

No, not at all.

Mum deserves this.

And I deserve to have a break from men.

With a love life as complicated as mine, it's almost a wonder I don't have a reality television crew following me around because I'd certainly offer them more drama than some of the other relationships that get broadcast. But it'll be a while until I let another man get close to me again, although I have promised Mum and myself that I refuse to let my prior experiences make me shy away from love in the future. I'm aware that none of what has happened before is my fault. I didn't ask to be targeted by a dangerous male with ulterior motives. I'm just a normal woman looking for normal things. Love. Security. Passion. I'm sure I'll find it one day and when I do, I'll get everything I deserve.

Next time, I will get the real wedding, a real house and after that, maybe I'll have a daughter of my own.

Only then will I truly understand what I have put my mother through in her life.

For now, I'm going to relax and just let life happen rather than force anything, and I'm also going to make the most of being in this house while I can because very soon, somebody else will be living here. After the drama with Harvey, Mum made the decision to try and sell the home I grew up in, deciding that whilst the property held many happy memories, it held several bad ones too, and it was time for a change of scene. She believed a fresh start would do her good, and me too, and I agreed, which is why I didn't protest when she told me the plan to put this place on the market.

While it won't be difficult to walk away from this house and the memories of the bad men who have been inside here, like Daryl, Harvey and Kyle, it will be tougher to walk away from the memories of the truly good man who once occupied this home. But as Mum says, we carry the memory of Dad with us in our hearts, not in a house, and I will remember that every time I think back to this property I used to call home.

I'm proud of Mum for moving on, and moving on she is. Her date tonight is proof of that.

I hope it goes well for her.

She deserves happiness.

I wonder if she will find it tonight.

35

DAWN

The time for messing around is over. I've trialled several outfits and canvassed my daughter's opinion on each of them. I've put my hair into different styles before settling on the one I think accentuates my face the best. And I've put on so much make-up that I almost had to do a double-take when I saw my reflection because I didn't recognise the youthful-looking woman staring back at me. But none of that really matters as I begin my date tonight because while I might look my best, I know it will all come down to how I end up feeling.

Will I like this guy that my friend, Maggie, has set me up with?

And based on my tumultuous past, *will he like me?*

After going through the initial pleasantries and ordering our first drink, my date this evening, Chris, has made a good first impression. He is polite, dressed well and, as Maggie warned me, is devilishly handsome. I'm trying not to think too much about what he might be thinking of me as we briefly discuss our mutual friend and how she came to put us together this evening, and we both agree that whatever happens, we'll keep the gossiping to a minimum when Maggie requests a debrief afterwards. After that, we start discussing our jobs, a simple enough conversation topic on a first date, but no matter how well it goes, I can't help thinking about the thing that could mess this all up.

Chris knows about what I have been involved with before, in terms of Daryl and Kyle and Harvey and all the drama that came with that. Such a history screwed up my last date, and I'm wondering if the same thing is going to happen here. Will Chris suddenly get uncomfortable and leave like John did, or will he feign politeness and make out like he doesn't care about it but realise afterwards that he actually does and tell Maggie that he never wants to see her friend ever again?

Then, totally surprising me, Chris addresses the metaphorical elephant in the room.

'Look, there's no point in me pretending like I don't know that you're one of the most famous women in this town,' he says with a smile. 'You're like the biggest celebrity around here, and I can tell people have been looking over at you since we came out tonight.'

I glance around at the other tables in here and see that Chris is right. A few people are looking in my direction, although they all try to pretend like they're not when I catch them staring.

'But I just want you to know that I don't care about any of that,' Chris goes on, his smile growing warmer by the second. 'I know that none of what happened had anything to do with you and your daughter. It was just bad luck, plain and simple, just like it was bad luck that I accidentally stepped in a puddle outside my house when I was on my way to meet you here tonight, and now I can feel my wet sock inside my shoe.'

I laugh at that before Chris goes on.

'I don't care what any of the journalists have said about you or any of the people in this town who don't know the real you. I do, however, care about what Maggie has told me about you because she is one of your best friends, so she has the right to have an opinion. And her opinion is that you are one of the most decent, honest and friendly people she has ever met in her life, so that's good enough for me.'

I really appreciate what Chris has said, but just before I can thank him, he has one more thing to say.

'By the way, I'm sure you're aware that some men might be intimidated by a woman who has killed one man, caught a con man and defused a potential hostage situation in her own home, but trust me, I am not. What you have done in your life is nothing short of heroic, and you should be proud of yourself every day for protecting your daughter so fiercely and so successfully. In my opinion, there's no more attractive quality in a woman than her being a good mother.'

Chris winks at me then, and that gesture, along with his good looks and confidence to even make a little speech like that, has me blushing, but in a very good way.

'Thank you,' I say to him, appreciating every word he has just said and feeling my own confidence growing now that I am sure I'm not wasting my time here tonight with yet another man who can't handle my past. Maybe John just felt insecure around me, and that's why he ran away from our date. But my current date has made it clear that he has no such insecurities, and with that potential obstacle now out of the way, the pair of us are free to get on with the rest of our date.

As time progresses, I quickly realise that for the first time since my husband passed away, I am seriously giving thought to the fact that I might have met a man who could go some way to filling that void in my life. I know nobody else can be Sean and make me feel like he did, but I deserve to give somebody else the chance, and I deserve to try it too. Ellie has said as much, and she wished me luck before I left the house tonight to go on this date, telling me she hoped it went well, that she couldn't wait to hear all about it and last but not least, that I deserved to be happy.

It's funny, but after so many years of worrying about my daughter, I feel like I am putting myself first for a rare change, and so far, it's going well. That is confirmed when, as our date concludes, simply because Chris and I have stayed so late together that the bar we are in is now closing, I am asked if I would like to do this again.

'Definitely,' I say to Chris as my taxi arrives, and he opens the door for me like a true gentleman.

'Wonderful,' he says with a smile before telling me that he'll be in touch, and I tell him that I'm looking forward to that.

Then I go to get into the taxi but just before I do, Chris leans in for a kiss, and surprising myself a little, I kiss him back, ever so lightly but enough to tell him that his feelings are reciprocated.

This budding relationship is already going somewhere.

I can only imagine how excited Maggie is going to be about this.

As the taxi moves on and I wave to Chris before he disappears from view, I am aware that Ellie is going to get an idea of how well things just went based on how much I am going to be smiling when I get home. But that's okay because I can't wait to tell her everything, and I know it will make her happy that I am happy.

As for my daughter and her own love life, I can only hope and pray that it will be third time lucky for her when it comes to her serious relationships. While she's had plenty of boyfriends before, the two men she has got closest to, Daryl and Kyle, have turned out to be disasters, and she deserves the third time to be different. But somebody else who might be thinking about a third time is Harvey, the man currently locked up in a prison about seventy miles away from here, where he has been held ever since he was arrested and sentenced for the murder of Kyle and the abduction of Ellie.

I'm well aware that the American man will be thinking about how Ellie escaped his son's clutches before escaping his own, and he might be wondering if he will get a third opportunity to do harm to her and, at the same time, me. The thought of one day getting a chance at revenge is most likely the only thing getting him through all the long days stretching ahead of him as he serves his time in a small cell with nothing for company but his own intrusive thoughts.

I know the plan is for him to serve his very long sentence for the crimes he committed in England before he will be deported back to the US.

But is that Harvey's plan?
Or has he got other ideas?
If so, what can Ellie and I do about it?

EPILOGUE

HARVEY

There are quite a few differences between British and American prisons, but the main point of them is the same - keep criminals locked away with very little to do until they are deemed safe enough to be released back into society. It doesn't really matter which side of the Atlantic I am kept behind bars on because the outcome is the same: I'm stuck in a tiny cell with nothing but thoughts of revenge to occupy my mind.

I came so close to making Dawn and Ellie pay for taking Daryl's life. I had my chances, and I should have taken them. I could have easily killed Ellie, and then, even if Dawn had been able to outsmart me and have me arrested, she still would have suffered with the loss of her daughter. But I didn't quite get to complete what I wanted to do, and having unfinished business is never a good thing for a person to have. But it does provide me with enough fuel to get me out of bed every morning and face another grim day in this prison, and that's about the only thing I do have keeping me going as I face an extremely long sentence. I'll be a very old man by the time I get out of here, and I'm sure to be swiftly deported back to the States once my sentence is served. But if the police, the prison authorities and, most importantly, that mother and daughter duo, think that means this is over then they are sadly mistaken.

This will only be over when I say it is.

While Dawn and Ellie get on with whatever daily chores they have to take care of on the outside world, I'm occupied with the job I have been given in this prison. I'm one of the prisoners selected to work in the laundrette, which means several hours a week of my sentence are spent in a hot, steamy room, listening to large tumble dryers while I load and unload huge piles of washing and fold it all into baskets. It's boring, monotonous and mind-numbing work, but I tend to get through it by fantasising about a day when I'm no longer in this place and when I can inflict pain on my enemies.

What else have I got?

It's during another one of my fantasies, my mind lost to a vivid daydream about hurting Dawn and Ellie, when I'm suddenly interrupted by one of my fellow inmates who asks me to take a basket of sheets to the airing cupboard just outside the main laundrette. The inmate who's asking, a guy called Kieran with a small scar beneath his left eye that I heard he got from another inmate in here, is not somebody to argue with, so I do as I'm told.

Picking up the basket, I carry it out of the laundrette, passing several of my fellow inmates as I go, as well as a couple of prison wardens who are overseeing everything that is happening in here. But as I reach the airing cupboard, there are no wardens in sight, and that allows me to have a moment to rest before I go back to work.

After putting the basket down, I initially think that I've been lucky to end up in this walk-in cupboard because everyone else is toiling away out there in that hot laundrette while I'm in this cooler space away from the condescending stares of the wardens. But I'm not feeling lucky when I see Kieran enter the airing cupboard behind me, and when he closes the door, I start to worry something is wrong.

'What are you doing?' I ask him, wondering why he would feel the need to close the door behind him.

'What I've been asked to do,' comes the confusing but also very chilling reply before I see Kieran take out what looks like a shiv that was hidden inside his own basket of laundry.

Suddenly realising that I'm in a very dangerous situation with a very dangerous prisoner, I try to leave, but Kieran blocks my path, and it's clear that the only way out of here is to go through him. But he has a deadly weapon while I don't, and as I stare at the sharp end of the blade, I am terrified it is about to be used on me.

'Wait, what have I ever done to you?' I ask Kieran, desperate to know why I have suddenly found myself with an enemy in this place.

'You've done nothing to me,' he replies. 'But you've done a lot to Dawn and Ellie.'

The names of those two women turn my blood cold.

'What have they got to do with this?' I ask, failing to see how they can be connected to the man with the scar on his face who has been an inmate in here for longer than I have and who is supposed to stay in here longer than me too.

'Well, they're the ones who have paid my family £5,000 for me to do this to you,' Kieran replies before he steps forward and sticks the sharp weapon into my stomach.

I try to fight back, but there's not much room for me in this enclosed space to manoeuvre myself out of harm's way, and as the second blow is dealt, I see lots of blood spilling out from beneath my uniform and onto the floor by my feet. I can also taste blood in my mouth, and by the time I have been stabbed a third time, I am losing my strength and find myself collapsing to the floor.

As I fight for my life, Kieran is quickly down on the ground, kneeling over me and stabbing me again whilst he tells me exactly what is happening.

'They found out which prison wing you were in from the news reports. Then they found out which inmates might be willing to do a little dirty work for them in exchange for money. You see, I'm never getting out of this place, but I have children to support on the outside, and that money they are giving to my family will go a long way to helping them. Dawn and Ellie have paid me to do this to you today, and before you die, they wanted you to know that this is over, and now they never have to worry about you coming for them again.'

That's the second-to-last thing I ever hear as Kieran stops stabbing me and gets back to his feet before walking away, leaving the bloodied shiv lying beside me on the ground. The last thing I hear is the door to this airing cupboard close, and as I'm left alone, I breathe my very last breath, aware of one very disturbing thing.

Dawn and Ellie have outsmarted me.

They have killed me before I could get out and try and kill them again.

I guess a mother's love for her child really does know no bounds.

THE END

Thank you for reading

If you would like to receive a FREE copy of my psychological thriller 'Just One Second', then you can find the link to the book at my website www.danielhurstbooks.com

Thank you for reading *My Daughter's Husband,* the sequel to my bestselling book, *My Daughter's Boyfriend.* I hope you enjoyed revisiting the characters of Dawn, Ellie and Harvey, as well as meeting new ones. I'm sure we can all agree that after these two stories, Dawn and Ellie are due some good luck with the men in their lives!

If you have enjoyed this psychological thriller, then you'll be pleased to know that I have several more stories in this genre, and you can find a list of my titles on the next page. These include my most popular book *Til Death Do Us Part*, which has a twist that very few people have been able to predict; *The Doctor's Wife*, which became the #1 selling book in the UK Kindle Store in February 2023, and its sequel, *The Doctor's Widow*.

ALSO BY DANIEL HURST

TIL DEATH DO US PART
THE DOCTOR'S WIFE
THE DOCTOR'S WIDOW
THE PASSENGER
WE USED TO LIVE HERE
MY DAUGHTER'S BOYFRIEND
THE INTRUDER
WHAT MY FAMILY SAW
THE HOLIDAY HOME
MY HUSBAND'S MISTAKE
THE BRIDE TO BE
HER LAST HOUR
THE PERFECT ESCAPE
RUN AWAY WITH ME
THE RIVALS
WE TELL NO ONE
THE WOMAN AT THE DOOR
HE WAS A LIAR
THE BROKEN VOWS
THE WRONG WOMAN
NO TIME TO BE ALONE
THE TUTOR
THE NEIGHBOURS
THE BREAK
THE ROLE MODEL
THE BOYFRIEND
THE PROMOTION
THE NEW FRIENDS
THE ACCIDENT

(All books available now on Amazon and Kindle Unlimited – read on to learn a little more about selected titles…)

TIL DEATH DO US PART

What if your husband was your worst enemy?

Megan thinks that she has the perfect husband and the perfect life. Craig works all day so that she doesn't have to, leaving her free to relax in their beautiful and secluded country home. But when she starts to long for friends and purpose again, Megan applies for a job in London, much to her husband's disappointment. She thinks he is upset because she is unhappy. But she has no idea.

When Megan secretly attends an interview and meets a recruiter for a drink, Craig decides it is time to act. Locking her away in their home, Megan realises that her husband never had her best interests at heart. Worse, they didn't meet by accident. Craig has been planning it all from the start.

As Megan is kept shut away from the world with only somebody else's diary for company, she starts to uncover the lies, the secrets, and the fact that she isn't actually Craig's first wife after all...

THE DOCTOR'S WIFE

The UK Kindle Store #1 Bestseller!

He thinks his secret is safe. But she knows the truth…

My husband is a doctor. He's smart and charming and everybody trusts him. **Except me.**

On the surface, it looks like I have it all – the perfect marriage, the perfect husband, the perfect life. But it's far from the truth. **Doctor Drew Devlin** is not the respectable figure he makes out to be. The reason we moved to this beautiful, old property with a gorgeous view of the sea was because we needed to put our past behind us. It should've been a fresh start for us both.

Except I've discovered my husband has been lying to me again. He's using the power he has in his job to mess with people's lives, and to get exactly what he wants – no matter who it hurts. But he's underestimated me. I've had plenty of time, in this big, isolated house, to think about all of his mistakes. *And my husband has no idea what's about to happen next…*

THE PASSENGER

She takes the same train every day. But this is a journey she will never forget…

Amanda is a hard-working single mum, focused on her job and her daughter, Louise. But it's also time she did something for herself, and after saving for years, she is now close to quitting her dreary 9-5 and following her dream.

But then, on her usual commute home from London to Brighton, she meets a charming stranger – a man who seems to know everything about her. Then he delivers an ultimatum. She needs to give him the code to her safe where she keeps her savings before they reach Brighton – or she will never see Louise again.

Amanda is horrified, but while she knows the threat is real, she can't give him the code. That's because the safe contains something other than her money. It holds a secret. *A secret so terrible it will destroy both her's and her daughter's life if it ever gets out…*

THE WOMAN AT THE DOOR

It was a perfect Saturday night. ***Until she knocked on the door...***

Rebecca and Sam are happily married and enjoying a typical Saturday night until a knock at the door changes everything. There's a woman outside, and she has something to say. Something that will change the happy couple's relationship forever...

With their marriage thrown into turmoil, Rebecca no longer knows who to trust, while Sam is determined to find out who that woman was and why she came to their house. But the problem is that he doesn't know who she is and why she has targeted them.

Desperate to save his marriage, Sam is willing to do anything to find the truth, even if it means breaking the law. But as time goes by and things only seem to get worse, it looks like he could lose Rebecca forever.

THE NEIGHBOURS

It seemed like the perfect house on the perfect street. *Until they met the neighbours...*

Happily married couple, Katie and Sean, have plenty to look forward to as they move into their new home and plan for the future. But then they meet two of their new neighbours, and everything on their quiet street suddenly doesn't seem as desirable as it did before.

Having been warned about the other neighbours and their adulterous and criminal ways, Katie and Sean realise that they are going to have to be on their guard if they want to make their time here a happy one.

But some of the other neighbours seem so nice, and that's why they choose to ignore the warning and get friendly with the rest of the people on the street. *And that is why their marriage will never be the same again...*

THE TUTOR

What if you invited danger into your home?

Amy is a loving wife and mother to her husband, Nick, and her two children, Michael and Bella. It's that dedication to her family that causes her to seek help for her teenage son when it becomes apparent that he is going to fail his end of school exams.

Enlisting the help of a professional tutor, Amy is certain that she is doing the best thing for her son and, indeed, her family. But when she discovers that there is more to this tutor than meets the eye, it is already too late.

With the rest of her family enamoured by the tutor, Amy is the only one who can see that there is something not quite right about her. But as the tutor becomes more involved in Amy's family, it's not just the present that is threatened. Secrets from the past are exposed too, and by the time everything is out in the open, Amy isn't just worried about her son and his exams anymore. She is worried for the survival of her entire family.

HE WAS A LIAR

What if you never really knew the man you loved?

Sarah is in a loving relationship with Paul, a seemingly perfect man who she is hoping to marry and start a family with one day, until his sudden death sends her into a world of pain.

Trying to come to terms with her loss, Sarah finds comfort in going through some of Paul's old things, including his laptop and his emails. But after finding something troubling, Sarah begins to learn things about Paul that she never knew before, and it turns out he wasn't as perfect as she thought. But as she unravels more about his secretive past, she ends up not only learning things that break her heart, but things that the police will be interested to know too.

Sarah can't believe what she has discovered. But it's only when she keeps digging that she realises it's not just her late boyfriend's secrets that are contained on the laptop. Other people's secrets are too, and they aren't dead, which means they will do anything to protect them.

RUN AWAY WITH ME

What if your partner was wanted by the police?

Laura is feeling content with her life. She is married, she has a good home, and she is due to give birth to her first child any day now. But her perfect world is shattered when her husband comes home flustered and afraid. He's made a terrible mistake. He's done a bad thing. *And now the police are going to be looking for him.*

There's only one way out of this. He wants to run. *But he won't go without his wife…*

Laura knows it is wrong. She knows they should stay and face the music. But she doesn't want to lose her man. She can't raise this baby alone. *So she agrees to go with him.* But life on the run is stressful and unpredictable, and as time goes by, Laura worries she has made a terrible mistake. They should never have ran. But it's too late for that now. Her life is ruined. The only question is: *how will it end?*

THE ROLE MODEL

She raised her. Now she must help her…

Heather is a single mum who has always done what's best for her daughter, Chloe. From childhood up to the age of seventeen, Chloe has been no trouble. That is until one night when she calls her mother with some shocking news. There's been an accident. *And now there's a dead body…*

As always, Heather puts her daughter's safety before all else, but this might be one time when she goes too far. Instead of calling the emergency services, Heather hides the body, saving her daughter from police interviews and public outcry.

But as she well knows, everything she does has an impact on her child's behaviour, and as time goes on and the pair struggle to keep their sordid secret hidden, Heather begins to think that she hasn't been such a good mum after all. *In fact, she might have been the worst role model ever…*

THE BROKEN VOWS

He broke his word to her. Now she wants revenge…

Alison is happily married to Graham, or at least she is until she finds out that he has been cheating on her. Graham has broken the vows he made on his wedding day. How could he do it? It takes Alison a while to figure it out, but at least she has time on her side. *Only that is where she is wrong.*

A devastating diagnosis means the clock is ticking down on her life now, and if she wants revenge on her cheating partner, then she is going to have to act fast. Alison does just that, implementing a dangerous and deadly plan, and it's one that will have far reaching consequences for several people, including her clueless husband.

WE USED TO LIVE HERE

How much do you know about your house?

When the Burgess family move into their 'forever' home, it seems like they are set for many happy years together at their new address. Steph and Grant, along with their two children, Charlie and Amelia, settle into their new surroundings quickly. But then they receive a visit from a couple who claim to have lived in their house before and wish to have a look around for old times' sake. They seem pleasant and plausible, so Steph invites them in. And that's when things start to change…

It's not long after the peculiar visit when the homeowners start to find evidence of the past all around their new home as they redecorate. But it's the discovery of a hidden wall containing several troubling messages that really sends Steph into a spin, and after digging deeper into the history of the house a little more, she learns it is connected to a shocking crime from the past. *A crime that still remains unsolved...*

Every house has secrets. But some don't stay buried forever…

THE 20 MINUTES SERIES

What readers are saying:

"If you like people-watching, then you will love these books!"

"The psychological insight was fascinating, the stories were absorbing and the characters were 3D. I absolutely loved it."

"The books in this series are an incredibly easy read, you become invested in the lives of the characters so easily, and I am eager to know more and more. Roll on the next book."

THE 20 MINUTES SERIES (in order)

20 MINUTES ON THE TUBE
20 MINUTES LATER
20 MINUTES IN THE PARK
20 MINUTES ON HOLIDAY
20 MINUTES BY THE THAMES
20 MINUTES AT HALLOWEEN
20 MINUTES AROUND THE BONFIRE
20 MINUTES BEFORE CHRISTMAS
20 MINUTES OF VALENTINE'S DAY
20 MINUTES TO CHANGE A LIFE
20 MINUTES IN LAS VEGAS

20 MINUTES IN THE DESERT
20 MINUTES ON THE ROAD
20 MINUTES BEFORE THE WEDDING
20 MINUTES IN COURT
20 MINUTES BEHIND BARS
20 MINUTES TO MIDNIGHT
20 MINUTES BEFORE TAKE OFF
20 MINUTES IN THE AIR
20 MINUTES UNTIL IT'S OVER

About The Author

Daniel Hurst lives in the Northwest of England with his wife, Harriet, and daughter, Penny, and if that doesn't make him lucky enough, he considers himself extremely fortunate to be able to write stories every day for his readers.

You can visit him at his online home www.danielhurstbooks.com

You can connect with Daniel on Facebook at www.facebook.com/danielhurstbooks or on Instagram at www.instagram.com/danielhurstbooks

He is always happy to receive emails from readers at daniel@danielhurstbooks.com and replies to every single one.

Thank you for reading.

Daniel

MY DAUGHTER'S HUSBAND by Daniel Hurst published by Daniel Hurst Books Limited, The Coach House, 31 View Road, Rainhill, Merseyside, L35 0LF

Front Cover Design by 100Covers